FIX ME

PART 1
-
SPRING

CHAPTER ONE

Why am I not wearing black? Why isn't anyone wearing black? What is wrong with me? Does it always smell like this in here? I feel sick. Why are people laughing? I want to go home. I can't though. He probably won't answer if I call. To be honest, if I were to call myself right now, I wouldn't answer either. Is it always this cold in here? The sound of bottles popping open makes me feel nauseated. What are they even laughing about? Are they high? I guess so – it's already 2 pm.

I move from the couch somehow, without attracting any attention from the others – even Adam. My room – or our room – is warmer, the smoke in the air is thicker in here, probably because the air has not been able to escape with the windows and door shut. My heart is beating fast – too fast. Why is my heart even beating? Wouldn't it be nice if it were to just stop? I cough. The smoke is creeping down my throat. I can't breathe. I'm about to fall over, but I am holding on tight to the wall. It's damp. Why is the wall damp? I manage to lie down on the bed – the sheets covered in weed and alcohol stains. This is disgusting!

What's the time? My body feels heavy and warm. I take my phone out of my jeans' pocket. 4 pm. A boy walks into the room. It's Adam. "Come on, Olly. Come and do shots with me!"

My head hurts so bad, and I feel dizzy. "I'll come in two minutes, babe," I answer. I am now feeling quite grossed out by myself. *Babe?* How lame. I don't even like him. Nonetheless, the reply apparently works, because he turns around and leaves the room.

There's a big bag underneath the bed – just what I'm looking for to put some of my clothes in. I now take some money lying on the table and put them in my pocket – there isn't much. I take my phone too and then open the window with my free hand. I'm nervous. Why is the window so dusty? Oh, probably because we haven't cleaned it at all since we moved in three years ago. I throw the bag out of the window. It lands on the fire escape.

"Olly, when are you coming?" Adam shouts from the living room. I climb out of the window and close it after me. My heart is beating so fast, and my palms are sweating. The stairs seem endless as I run down them with the bag over my shoulder – step after step, ah, the stairs seem endless. Finally, I can feel the ground under them. My legs give up, and I land hard on the sidewalk knees first. Fuck. I can feel my tears trickling down now.

I manage to get my phone out of my pocket. 11% left. My fingers are shaking as I am trying to dial his number. I feel dizzy. My heart is beating fast. Something inside of me hopes he won't pick up. I hear his voice. My phone almost slips out of my hand.

A car drives up to the sidewalk, and he walks out. Dad. He comes up to me and looks at me straight in the eye.
"Are you drunk?" he asks coldly.

"I haven't had anything today," I reply and stare down at the ground to escape eye contact. He picks up my bag and puts it carefully in the trunk of the car. I try to stand up, but my legs are shaking underneath, and my knees are in pain. He helps me up and leads me to the passenger seat without saying anything.

The car journey is long. The radio is playing quietly in the background, but I'm not listening. The only thing I can hear is my heart pounding, like the sound of drums banging loudly in my ears. I'm not ready to go home and face my mom and younger brother — I just can't. Facing Dad has been hard enough, and we haven't even spoken much yet. My phone starts ringing. It's Adam. Dad looks over at me as I decline the call and then continues to look out of the windshield.

Which part of town is this? I mean... Just look at the big beautiful houses, with green lawns and nice cars parked out front. I can see the houses and the cars moving past us and out of sight. In a short while, were slowing down outside one such house. They moved a bit after I lost sight of them, but I didn't know where. I do now.

Dad pulls into the driveway and looks at me again. "It's Sam's 10th birthday today. Don't ruin it," he tells me firmly and gets out of the car. I do the same. I can't believe I missed three of Sam's birthdays. "Come and take your bag, will you?" he continues in a raw tone before taking out a beautiful cake from the trunk. They couldn't afford getting a cake like that when I turned 10, but I guess a lot has changed. I steal a glance at their house — it's huge and beautiful.

We walk up to the front door, and he unlocks it with a code. *Seriously?*

"Why is the door locked? Aren't they home?" We walk inside, and he places the cake on a counter in the hallway. There's a wide staircase to my left and a passage opening into what looks like the kitchen.

"They're in the garden with our neighbors," he tells me, "You can come and join us, but take a shower first in your bathroom and change into something that smells less of alcohol and drugs." This is surprising. I haven't been expecting an invitation.

"Hey...and don't touch the cake." He shouts as he walks through the house and leaves me standing alone.

"I like beer, not white frosting with sprinkles," I shout back, and I hear a little laugh from him. It has been a long time since I last heard him laugh. The door opens followed by the sound of people talking. It stops as soon as the door closes again.

Something suddenly strikes me – he didn't tell me where my room is. I try to shout after him, but he is already out in the garden. I'm not going out there yet. Instead, I will find out where my room is myself.

I walk up the big staircase and glance down a corridor with a few doors on either side. It's not as narrow as one may imagine. The corridor is really bright, probably because of the white walls and the big window at the end, with long, light blue curtains on each side. Mom definitely had too much to say. I can feel a smile curving around the corner of my lips. I haven't seen her in a very long time.

Are one of these rooms mine? This first one on my left must be my parents' room – there's a king-sized bed and old-looking flower-printed bedding. Again, I think Mom had had a bit too much to say. That honestly doesn't surprise me – she has always been such a control freak. At one point, I really thought about asking Dad why he had even married her. But, he had plenty of reason to kick me out already; it would have been stupid of me to add more.

The first door on the right is just a bathroom, then an office, and then Sam's room. There is one door to the left at the very end of the corridor. I open it, and whoa... there are stairs. Is there a whole other floor in this house? I drop my bag on the floor and walk up the stairs. It's like a corridor, a very small one, with a door on each side and no windows to light up the little space. The light emerging from the door at the end of the stairs lights up the small corridor. The walls are pale yellow, and the floor is covered with a dark gray carpet. It is clear that Mom has not renovated this part of the house.

I open the door on the left. It's only a cute little bathroom of a light peach color. I mean, everything in here is peach. I actually like it a bit; it's cute and small. Don't they use this part of the house? I open the other door, and there's my room. There are around twenty boxes with my name on them, stacked on top of each other. So, they have given me the whole loft? He did say *your* room and *your* bathroom. So, I guess this is *my* space. Sick.

The big window at the end of the room is curtained with long, white, see-through drapes. Through the drapes, I can see the garden – it is bigger than I thought it would be when I had earlier seen the house out front

I open the window, and the delicious smell of barbecue hits me. Looking down again, I can see some people sitting around a long, wooden garden table. Dad and another man are standing beside the grill. It looks surprisingly chilled. I don't like barbecues or dinners like these at all. There are these unwritten rules about how to act, and I follow them like the idiot that I am. Well, everybody follows it. Most people don't even notice they exist...and those who do – like me – follow them anyway. You know, rules like don't eat, laugh, or talk too loudly, don't eat too much but taste a bit of everything, and the last one – and probably the most important one, in my mom's opinion – don't show up without some kind of hostess gift. It's stupid.

A boy is screaming at my dad. Sam. He is standing at the end of the garden and playing soccer with himself. He looks so different. "Dad! Look at me!" Sam shouts, performing a trick with the soccer ball, and the two men smile at him. Then, they continue their conversation beside the barbeque. Sam and I used to play soccer in the old garden for hours – I remember it so clearly –. Back then, we lived in a small house with a very small garden. It was probably as big as my new room, but it was alright. We didn't care...especially not Sam. I couldn't stop caring after I turned fourteen. From thereon, everything fell apart I guess.

I began looking at the other kids differently; I began focusing on how much money their parents probably earned. I also began experimenting with my sexuality, which didn't help me at all. I was pretty weird. I guess that's why I had just one friend left in my class when I finished primary school. Luckily, I had some friends outside of school – Adam was one of them. I don't want to think more about the past right now...or even what happened just earlier today. I'm going to my little brother's 10th birthday, and maybe, I'll even stay at my family's house if I don't mess this dinner up. But first, I have to shower and change into clothes that don't smell like three years of bad habits.

I am out of the shower, and I check my phone. 5% left. It is 5.30 pm and there are four missed calls from Adam, two from Jacob, and a message from Britney asking where the hell I am. Great. I wrap a towel around my waist and walk out of the bathroom and into my room. The boxes are filled with all my old stuff. I'm not in the mood for looking through them right now. Instead, I'll just focus on finding the ones that contain clothing.

Some of my old clothes are horrible, and some are not. One thing is clear though – my style has changed a lot. I put on a pair of black jeans and a dark green jumper. There's a long mirror hanging on the other side of the door. Looking at my reflection, it seems I've clearly lost a good amount of weight – My old clothes are now way too big for my little body. My hair is a mess – brown, curly, and still a bit wet from the shower. It's impossible to fix it. Should I take my nose ring out? I know how much my mom will hate it. Even though she hasn't seen it before, I just know she will. Dad didn't react on it...or on my new style in general; also, I think that he expected something much worse than a nose ring and some vintage-looking clothes. Let's keep it in though. I need something familiar. *Everything* around feels new.

I walk out of the door. I'm feeling nervous. I'm walking the same way I saw Dad go through the house, following the sound of people talking. This part of the house is quite fancy – an open kitchen, a long dining table, and a nice lounge at the back. Hey, there's even that piano in the corner I used to play. My heart is beating like earlier, and I feel a little dizzy. This is great. I could really use a cigarette or a beer right now. It'll calm me down. I can't see how many people are out there because of the light curtains.

I open the door to the terrace. The voices are getting more audible now. Sam is the first one to spot me as I show up behind the door. He is getting up from his chair and running toward me. His hug is tight... and surprisingly familiar. He has grown so much. Mom's getting up too.

"Happy birthday," I tell him. He's smiling at me. Okay, now I feel a little bad about not having a present or anything. Although, he doesn't seem to care. Wait... why do I suddenly care? Sam goes back to his chair, and Mom walks closer to me. I'm nervous. Okay, she's cupping my face with her motherly hands and is stroking my skin gently with her thumb. I'm sweating. Her eyes are watering, and I can see that she's biting her lower lip.

"Did you find your room?" she asks, giving my shoulders a squeeze before letting them fall to her sides. I nod. I cannot really trust my voice right now. It's so overwhelming to see her again after so long.

I walk around the table and shake hands. First, Judy, a woman around the same age as my mom, then Charles, Judy's husband, then Katy, their little girl, then this beautiful girl Sia, who I guess is around my age, and then the last stranger sitting at the end of the table. He is a boy, around my age as well, who I'm assuming is Sia's boyfriend. He almost ignores me as I stick my hand out, but Sia kicks his leg underneath the table. He shakes my hand without looking at my face. Does he think I'm after his girlfriend or something?

They have left a chair for me beside my mom and in front of Judy. That's nice... I'm as far away from the boy as possible.

"Olly, can I ask you something?" Sia asks shortly after the food is served.

"Sure, what's up?" I answer and try my best to ignore the fact that the boy's eyes are hunting me down.

"It is just because... I'm pretty sure I've seen you before,"

"Okay... where?" I ask. I'm pretty sure I haven't seen her before.

"In the town with that guy, what's his name...?" She tries to recall the name she was looking for. Now the boy is looking me straight in the eye, and he spits: "Adam." Like if it is the Devil's name, and we are sitting in God's house.

"Yeah, of course!" Sia says loudly. I feel sick. Of course, they know who he is. I was really hoping that I could just have a break from him at this point. But, I guess it's not possible.

"Thank you, Jaden," Sia says and looks at Jaden, who is staring down at his plate. Jaden? Is that his name? Why does it sound so familiar?

"Adam? Wasn't he that guy you dated?" Mom asks, God, there are *people* around the table. Ugh.

"Yes, and we are still kind of dating, Mom" I reply, feeling gross. I don't want to be with him anymore, but I can't really say that we aren't together before actually breaking up with him.

"Oh. So, is he one of your roommates?" Dad asks me. He can't fully understand what we are talking about – it's on his face. I don't judge him though. I haven't really given him a chance to follow my life over the last few years.

"Yes, Dad, he *was* my roommate."

"Was?" Mom asks, and I look down on my plate. I had promised Dad that I wouldn't fuck this evening up. I don't know if it's a good idea to mention it right now.

"Has Adam moved out of your apartment?" Dad asks. He's clearly confused now. The others around the table are listening. God, this is uncomfortable.

"No. Adam still lives in the apartment with the others. I'm moving out..." I trail off.

Sam suddenly says, "Are you coming back home?" He looks so happy and smiles at me, but with a little nervousness hiding behind that big bright smile. He's probably scared that I'm going to say no.

"So, are you?" Mom asks me, and I feel all their eyes on me.

"Yeah... if I may?" A second later, I feel my mom's embrace from the side.

"Of course, you can, Olly," Dad answers. They seem almost relieved about me moving back home. That wasn't what I had expected.

We have finished dinner now. I didn't really say anything – just sat back in the chair and listened to the others talk about work and life in general. I heard that Dad is still working in the office in town, with Charles, but is getting paid a lot better. Also, Mom has become the executive in the theatre just out of town. That is surprising. I knew she was studying something back then, but I never asked what. I feel so stupid for not knowing.

"Olly and Jaden, can you two maybe get the cake?" Charles asks and I glance over at Jaden. He is staring at me with disgust. I don't get why he can't stand me.

"I'll get it myself. It didn't look that heavy," I answer and get up from my chair.

"I will help you," Sia offers and gets up too. She looks pissed at Jaden. He is just ignoring her. What an idiot. How can such a beautiful girl be with an asshole like him? She's probably with him because of his physical appearance. I must admit that he is a good-looking dude, although his shitty personality outshines it.

Sia and I walk inside the house. I can hear Charles telling Jaden that he should pack his attitude away or leave. I can't hear an answer coming from Jaden though because Sia's just started talking.

"Not to be rude or anything, but is that Adam guy even nice?" She looks at me with pity in her eyes and then down at her shoes.

"He is nicer that Jaden," I answer. Ouch! That came out a bit colder than expected. But, how *could* she ask that, when her boyfriend is an idiot too?

"He is my twin. It's not my choice to be around him." Twin? Now, I'm *really* confused.

"Is Jaden your brother?" I ask, feeling quite stupid.

"Yeah, and he is actually not that bad normally." Why does she stick up for him? He is an asshole.

"Okay, so he just can't stand me?"

"I don't know what his problem is, to be honest. But, I do know that you two will become friends at some point." Sia answers confidently. I don't want to try to become his friend, and I can only imagine him feeling the same way.

We get the cake from the counter and walk back in silence. Sia is cool enough; I just hope her brother won't talk her out of hanging out with me.

So, the birthday song for Sam and the cake-eating is done. I didn't enjoy that much – sweets aren't really my thing. Now, we are just sitting and talking with blankets around us that Mom got for us all. It's getting pretty chilly out here... probably because it's spring. Mom has an arm around me. When was the last time this had happened? It feels nice though.

Suddenly, Jaden decides to say something. To *me*, of course.

"So, you are pretty close to Adam, right?" he starts. Ugh! I was feeling so at ease. Why does he have to ruin it for me?

"Um... yeah, I guess. Why?" I answer. I'm feeling a little nervous with this sudden attention towards me. What is he up to?

"Then you knew Meghan too, right?" He asks, looking so innocent. How can he even bring that up? Asshole. Doesn't that guy have any respect?

"Jaden, don't you dare," Sia involves herself. She's looking directly at Jaden now. Does she also know about Meghan? I feel like throwing up, and my palms are sweating.

"Yes, I did," is all I can answer. My stomach turns, and my head is in a mess. Where is he going with this?

"So, were you at her funeral this morning?" Jaden continues. Anger is brewing in my veins. I can feel tears forming in my eyes, but I ignore them. Why didn't we go? She didn't deserve to get buried alone. Mom looks worriedly at me, while Charles tells Jaden to go inside and into his room. Jaden doesn't stop at this. His eyes are glued to me.

"Is it true that she was raped, or is that just something you guys made up for a bit more attention? I mean, it looks great on Britney's campaign." I can feel this violent wave of frustration rush through my body. My eyes are no longer dry. Charles gets up from his chair and yells at Jaden that he must go now, and thankfully, he does. I get up to leave too, and my eyes meet Sam's, full of confusion – his birthday is ruined. I could really use a cigarette right now. I should have just stayed away.

I take my bag with me upstairs. It was lying on the floor in the corridor, where I'd left it earlier. *Earlier.* I wish I could go back to earlier.

I look through my bag. There is not one cigarette. Fuck. I lie down on the bed. I can still taste the beer in my mouth. I had been drinking a few today. How could I forget the cigarettes on the table? I can picture the packet of cigarettes lying on the nightstand beside our bed in the apartment. What a shitty night!

CHAPTER TWO

Iwake up with an annoying headache and five missed calls from Adam. Can't that boy please just leave me alone? I'm trying to move on. I wish I hadn't put my phone in the charger before going to sleep last night. Now, I have 100% and no excuse not to call him back. What should I even say to him? I don't want to talk to him.

My body is tired, and my urge to smoke a bunch of cigarettes is getting crazy. I will respond to Adam's calls later today. I get up from the bed. Fuck. I'm still wearing the same clothes I had on last night. I am so exhausted. I stretch and rub my eyes. I don't need to change yet.

I walk downstairs. Mom and Dad are talking in the kitchen, and Sam is watching TV.

"Good morning Olly, are you okay after last night?" Mom asks, worried. I shrug, not knowing what to say. I'm not okay, but I don't want their pity.

"I had hoped that you and Jaden would bond. But, maybe another time, right?" Mom continues. She stacks some papers lying all over the counter. Why are they so optimistic? I don't want to become friends with that idiot.

"He clearly couldn't even stand looking at me. How the fuck would we ever get to know each other!" I shout, feeling quite upset and maybe a little hurt. Dad looks angry about my shouting.

I walk out into the hallway and slip on my sneakers.

"Where are you going?" Dad asks, leaning against the opening, with his arms crossed over each other.

"Into town," I bite back. I'm not interested in having my parents check up on me. I can't believe I'm eighteen and have moved back home to my parents'.

The town is quiet this morning. It's Sunday and only 8 am. When I was little, my parents, baby Sam, and I used to come to this part of town on Sundays. I remember loving the cute little stores and the fancy cafés we never visited. Now they live in this area, like they're literally a five-minute walk away from midtown.

My stomach is churning...but I need to find a store first. I can get some cigarettes there. Anxiety is frothing inside of me – I ignore it. The woman behind the counter looks nice. I take the crumpled dollars out of my jeans' pocket and ask for the cheapest kind they have.

I get out of the store and rip the plastic packaging off. I'm Lucky – There's a lighter in my bomber jacket. Ah, I love the kick out of smoke rushing down my throat...the calm feeling in my body. Let me close my eyes – I want to focus fully on my senses. Why is that dog barking? Nothing can ruin my mood though. The best thing in the world is an early cigarette. I'll smoke one more. I must also find some food soon...all the eateries get filled up. There's still an hour or so. It's Sunday, remember?

I can really use some breakfast...maybe some beer too. I walk into a sweet little café – Brooks Café. Mmm... the smell is delicious. Freshly brewed coffee. The walls are all light yellow. But, who's that woman coming over to me? Judy?

"Olly, what a surprise!" Judy greets me with a tight hug. She leads me to a little two-person table and sits down in front of me. She tells me that her family owns the café.
"That's awesome. It's really nice in here," I tell her and look around.
"Thank you. Now, what can I get for you, sweetie?" she asks and gets up. I like her. The menu on the table is filled with different names and numbers. Boy, am I really going to have to choose something from here? I sigh and put the menu to the side.
"Surprise me," I tell her, and she smiles at me again. This woman is just one big smile, I guess. She promises me that the food will be ready very soon and disappears through a little door behind the counter. I guess it leads to the kitchen.
   A group of teens around my age walks into the café and sits down in a big booth in the corner. I've seen a few of them before, probably in the local club. They look pretty cool. God, Olly look away – you don't want to look like some freak sitting at the other end of the café staring at them.

Judy comes back from the kitchen with my food and smiles at the teens sitting in the corner, before placing a lot of small brunch dishes and a glass of orange juice on my table. She tells me that it is Jaden who's decided and cooked the food for me. Of course, Jaden is here. Asshole. I don't think I would trust this food if it wasn't for Judy coming with it. The kitchen door opens, and I see Jaden walk over to the group. How awkward. Judy follows my eyes.
"They are actually really nice...Jaden included," she whispers and smiles one last time, before turning around and disappearing into the kitchen.

I look at the food. Wow, he's actually done a great job; I can only cross my fingers and hope that it isn't poisoned.

I look at them sometimes. My eyes meet Jaden's, but then I look down at my food or phone again. They are probably talking about me. Jaden must be telling them that I am dating Adam and that I was one of that slut Meghan's friends. I can't say for sure...but, why wouldn't he? It's a great story – the weirdo over there is my new neighbor. That's what they are laughing at between bites of food.

Jaden walks back into the kitchen after hanging out with them for a while. One of the girls gets up and walks directly to my table. Oh no! She sits down in front of me and smiles warmly. What's going on? Did I stare too much?

"Hi, my name is Leah," She holds her hand out for me to shake it.

"Olly," I respond, shaking her hand, feeling very awkward.

"I know, Jaden told me." I was right; they *did* talk about me. She smiles like Judy – very big, very bright.

"Leah, let Olly eat in peace," Sia says from behind the counter, and they both chuckle. They seem to be pretty good friends. Hey, wait. Is Sia here too? She walks over and hugs me. She smells strongly of women's perfume and mint.

"Have you asked Olly to come to the party?" Leah whispers in Sia's ear as they embrace each other. I probably shouldn't have heard that. Sia shakes her head. What party? I wonder what party they're talking about, but I'm interrupted by Sia talking to me.

"Hey, Jaden and I are having a party at our house on Friday, and I would love to see you there." She wants me to come, but what about Jaden? I am about to ask them, but Leah already read my face.

"I will get Arden to talk to Jaden," she tells Sia and thanks her. Who's Arden? And...why do I suddenly care?

CHAPTER THREE

The knocking on my door is getting louder and louder.

What the fuck! I get up and open. Sia? Oh yeah, she'd offered to help me yesterday with the unpacking.
"It's 12 noon, Olly. Why aren't you up yet?" she asks me and walks past me into the room. And of course, I see Jaden, The Devil, walking in after her. We both avoid eye contact. Cold wind. It's breezing in through the doorway with them. Shit! I'm almost completely exposed – just black briefs. There are some sweatpants in my bag. I'll put them on.

Sia is going through a box full of old pictures, papercuts, and collages from when I was little. I was a weird child. Sia is telling me how great and cute I was, but well, she's just being polite. I wasn't really good at anything particular. Jaden isn't doing much – just sitting on my bed, texting away on his phone. Why is he even here? This boy pisses me off.

I'm going through my old clothes. God, I had such bad taste back then. I get now why Adam didn't want to be seen in public with me. He always brought clothes from his closet when he would be coming by and before heading out. My parents hated it though. Mom loved my style. She was afraid that meeting Adam would change my personality. I see why she was worried now but back then it didn't really make any sense to me. Maybe, I just didn't want it to. I actually liked Adam – he is... err.. was my first love.

Having looked through the boxes, we are now writing down the things I need for my room – a lamp for my nightstand, new towels for my bathroom, blah blah blah – things I would never have noticed were missing if I hadn't gotten lots of help from Sia.

Sia has made my day so incredible. She reminds me of my old best friend...I haven't spoken to her in ages. All of this old stuff reminds me of her. I miss her. Well, that's alright; Sia's here now. But, she'll be here for only an hour more...She works on Mondays too. I'll offer to come and hang out with her... She won't get bored that way. She says the café is incredibly busy on weekdays... she won't get the time to talk to me anyway. Sad. I only asked because I'm going to be extremely bored myself tonight. What am I going to do with my life now?

Jaden is going to the bathroom. I say goodbye to Sia and close my door, That's lucky – I can avoid saying *goodbye* or *see you* to him. We both know that we would like to avoid the last one. His visit makes me a bit confused... like what the hell is he doing here? It's probably because Arden told him to. I still don't know who Arden is though, and I don't feel like having him around either. I won't try to become friends with him after what happened on Saturday night.

I put on my old bomber jacket and a white t-shirt that I found while rummaging through my old clothing. I grab the list and my phone and leave the room. *Jaden?* I almost jump in shock.

"You are still here?" I breathe out after the awkward encounter.

"Um, yeah. Where are you going?" he asks, confused, closing the bathroom door behind him. Did he plan on staying here without Sia? I wave the little piece of paper in my hand and explain that I'm going to the mall to buy things I need for my room.

"Oh, cool. Do you have a car?" he asks. Oh shit, my driver's license got seized last month, neither do I own a car... I used to drive Adam's one. How was I even planning to get to the mall?

"Can I drive you there?" Wow. Jaden's tone sounds, eerrr... *friendly*? Is he trying to be kind to me? What do I say? I can't say no. That would be awkward. Also, I really need to get these things.

"That would be nice, thanks," I answer politely, and we start walking down the stairs. This is weird.

His car is big. It's clear black and has dark leather seats. We both get inside it. He connects his phone to the car and chooses a song. Hey, that's the first thing I do as well.

This ride is awkward. Thank God for the loud music, it makes the silence less uncomfortable – it is like a sound barrier. He apparently loves R&B. I expected that, seeing his average style. You know the 'white t-shirt and black jeans with holes in the knees' kind? Not that it can't be sexy –*actually*, it works quite well for Jaden.

He's driving into the parking lot. Shit, this place is crowded. People – they always give me such a panic attack. I can feel my heart beating faster now – that same people anxiety again. Why didn't I think this through? My throat is dry – really dry. I see Jaden – he's trying to find a free spot. Should I ask him to drive me back home again? I lean my head back against the backrest. I'll just shut my eyes. I try to focus on my breathing. It only gets worse. Cars are honking at one another – so chaotic.

"Are you okay?" Jaden suddenly asks. Why is his voice so soft? I open my eyes. He has already parked. My head starts hurting. It makes me even more uncomfortable. I *hate* feeling like this. Jaden takes out a water bottle from the glovebox and holds it out for me. I skull it down. I can feel his eyes on me.

"Can we just sit here for a moment?" I ask through my groans. My head is pounding. And I feel dizzy.

"Of course, just relax... we don't have to hurry," he tells me, and I thank him. I rest my head on my knees and try to regulate my breathing. Is that Jaden's hand on my back? He must be feeling the slight trembles. Wow, I didn't think he would understand. He actually seems quite cool about this. This doesn't necessarily mean he's changed his opinion of me, though. Now's a good time to just get things cleared. I mean, let's at least try.

"Why do you hate me?" I am almost inaudible. He groans, annoyed.

"I don't actually hate you – I hate Adam," he explains and gives my back a gentle squeeze, and then quickly removes his hand. It's the first time there's someone with me during a panic episode. His touch his calming.

"What's your problem with Adam?" I ask, sitting up fully to face him.

"Everything about that breathing asshole is my problem," he spits. I am a little offended by it. Although, I can understand why he feels that way. Adam can be quite mean and controlling – there's a reason why I want to break up with him.

"Olly, I'm really sorry for being a dick the other night," he whispers and gives me a weak smile. I smile back. Maybe, Sia is going to be right after all. We sit like this for a bit.

"Are you ready to go inside?" he asks, pointing at the mall right in front of us. I nod, and we both get out of his car. Shit. I have to make sure none of Adam's friends see us together. That can be so much trouble.

"Hey if anyone who knows Adam sees us, I'm dead" I blurt out to Jaden.

"Hey, don't say that. No one is going to put as much as a finger on you," he speaks in a low tone as we walk toward the swing door.

"Okay, bad boy," I try to tease him. I know it's a cliché but Jaden saying that – that no one will be able to put a finger on me – it's... hot. I have heard rumors that Jaden Brooks is a pretty mean fighter – probably one of the reasons why Adam sees him as a threat.

We walk through the swing door at the mall and stop to look at the crowded streets with shops down the sides. I get a little anxious again, but I try to ignore it.

"What do you need to buy?" he asks with a calm voice and puts a hand on my shoulder.

"Just hand me the list. I will help you find the things on it. I come here pretty often and know where what is," he continues. I take the list out of my jacket pocket and hand it to him. He quickly checks the list and starts walking down a street.

He finds the things I need in different shops. Every time he walks up to a counter to pay, I offer to pay, and every time he just tells me, "You can just pay me back later." This is quite a relief actually – I don't like to pay and don't have enough money either. Jaden is chatting away with the man or woman behind the counter like it is the most natural thing ever. That's kind of a little admirable.

I haven't actually done much on this shopping spree. I've just been walking behind him and answering questions now and then about colors and sizes and carried the bags. We've bought lamps, towels, flower-scented soaps, and a little build-it-yourself closet in a big box that Jaden is carrying because I'm too weak, and also because Jaden is apparently quite muscular. His arm muscles are flexing when he is carrying the box.

I feel annoyed with the people around me – little things about people that shouldn't really matter. Great... More people are showing up. I'm much calmer now though... I'm calm, but hunger is kicking in. We've been here for around two hours now, and I still haven't had anything to eat yet.

"That's everything!" Jaden announces as we leave a little candle shop.

"Nice. Can we grab something to eat, maybe? My stomach is eating itself from the inside, and it doesn't feel nice," I explain, and Jaden chuckles. The chuckle's adorable

"Yeah, you don't have much stomach to begin with, so we better be quick," he jokes. We walk out with the bought items toward his car. We both don't want to eat in the mall because of all the people who have decided to come shopping on a Monday afternoon. Jaden tells me that he knows a lovely restaurant a few minutes away. So, we instead decide to drive there and eat.

The restaurant, to my disappointment, is packed, but Jaden, seeing that I was getting anxious again, calms me down and assures me that he has a plan. I don't know what that is, but I'm starving. So, I'm just going to trust him and follow him into the restaurant.

Jaden holds the door open for me. My nose is hit by the warm air and the delicious smell of fries. I'm so hungry. Jaden walks up to the counter, and whoa, a lot of guys are showing us up a staircase in the corner. Jaden is talking and laughing with them, but he looks back at me a few times. They are talking loudly about a soccer game. Apparently, Jaden made a *genius* goal last week. Not surprising – he does actually look like a stereotypical soccer player.

We go up the stairs, and Jaden begins introducing me to the group. They clearly have the same prejudices Jaden had the first time we met. A few of them look skeptical, but Jaden assures them with a firm gaze that I'm approved. They seem to trust him, seeing how they are trying to be nice to me. A tall one with tattoos down his bare arms even asks me how I'm doing.

I answer that I'm feeling pretty good, but on the inside, I want to run away. I couldn't feel more wrongly placed than in this *enemy territory*. I have seen a lot of them around in this town, and not because they were small-talking with my friends. Lucky for me, I haven't fought or argued with any of them – that's not really my style, but Adam has definitely been in a fight with at least half of them. I can assume that they know I'm with Adam, because both Jaden and Sia knew.

They leave Jaden and me alone, seated at a little wooden table. I can hear the noise of customers talking and employees shouting out to those waiting for their orders downstairs. I look around for the first time – a few more empty tables and no other people on this floor. Why don't they fill these tables up with customers? They're so packed downstairs, but up here, there is no one besides us.

Suddenly, it hits me why Jaden's name seemed so familiar. It stands on the list hanging in the apartment – a list of people Adam doesn't want us to mingle with. *Jaden Brooks*. I'm scared. I would never have had the guts to take Jaden with me to our apartment or pub– that would be too dangerous – then, what am I doing here?

Jaden interrupts my thoughts by asking if I have decided what to order yet. Stupid question. He knows I haven't looked at the menu even once yet. I pick it up from the table. What if Adam finds out about me being here? Fuck. I need to get out of here. I put the menu down and get up. Jaden looks at me, confused.

"I think it's best if I just buy a sandwich next door instead," I tell him. I am getting really anxious now. My palms are sweating. What have I gotten myself into? Jaden gets up from his chair too. Next moment, I see a girl coming up the stairs. She looks beautiful and gives me a sweet smile. Too sweet?

"Where is the bathroom?" I ask Jaden, and he points to a little door in the corner. I need to be alone.

There's no heat in the bathroom, and the walls are covered with cold, light blue tiles. I slide down the side of the wall behind the door after making sure that there's no one else here. My head is feeling heavy, probably because I still haven't eaten anything today.

The door opens slightly, and the girl I saw coming up the stairs earlier sticks her head inside. Her eyes catch mine, and she smiles warmly. What is she up to? She walks inside with a glass of water in her hand.

"Hey! I'm Arden," she says and hands me the glass of water. *She's* Arden.

"Hi, I'm Olly," I reply and glance down at the glass of water before gulping it down. I immediately feel so much better.

"Sia and Leah have been talking non-stop about you on skype. So, you must be a pretty big deal," she says, sitting down next to me.

"Not really," I answer and chuckle. What could they have possibly said about me? There's silence in the bathroom for a few seconds, and my stomach suddenly decides to protest. The loud churning reverberates as I try to cover my stomach with my arms. But, it doesn't help. How awkward.

"Why are you hiding in the bathroom? Is Jaden that tiring?" she asks and laughs. Her laugh is warm. It flaunts her glistening, beautiful teeth.

"No, he is fine. I guess I'm just feeling a bit anxious today." Why am I telling her this? Maybe because she's just so calming. I feel like I could talk to her for ages in here.

"Are you and Adam still a thing?" she suddenly asks. I hesitate.

"Kind of... though I don't really want to anymore," I blurt out. Fuck. Why did I say that? If Adam gets to know that I have said this, I'm so done.

"You really can't tell him," I tell her and look her in the eyes. She looks confused.

"Why would I do that? I hate Adam," she assures me and runs her fingers through my hair. I just know we will become good friends. She gets up from the cold floor. I'm tempted to ask a question. Should I ask? I don't know if I want to know the answer. Okay, I'm just going to.

"Why do Jaden and Adam hate each other so much?" I ask and immediately regret. She offers me a hand to get up.

"Because that asshole sent some of our friends to the hospital – kicked one in the face, smashed a bottle on another's head – and did some other vile stuff," she explains. My stomach is turning. I know that Adam can be violent, but he always refused to tell me the specifics of these situations – tried to hide it for me. "and that's why Jaden wants to hate you as well, but I can see why he's having a hard time doing that," she continues and smiles warmly at me. I blush a bit. I wish I could just be friends with this group instead of my own.

We leave the bathroom. Wow! All my worries seem to have disappeared. Jaden isn't at our table. Arden tells me that he's hanging out with the guys in the kitchen and that he has already ordered food for me. I sit down at the table, and she runs down the stairs. I'm left alone, which I do appreciate. I can still hear people talking downstairs, but that's not a bother. I'm calm. The silence is, of course, getting interrupted by my churning stomach again. I'm so damn hungry I can't even think clear anymore.

I can hear someone coming up the stairs. I turn around and see Jaden carrying two trays in his hands. He looks clumsy... and cute.

"Why didn't you ask someone to help you carry all that?" I ask and chuckle, as he carefully places the trays on the table. It looks delicious.

"I didn't want to make you all anxious again, so I thought it was better to let the guys stay downstairs," he explains, pushing one of the trays toward me. It has a burger with French fries, a cold beer, and a glass water with lemon and ice. My mouth is literally watering.

"What are you waiting for? Eat." Jaden says and throws a French fry into his mouth. Over the next few minutes, we're both just eating. Now and then, when I look up, our eyes meet; then, we both look down quickly. It's kind of weird how we hated each other the other day, and now, we are shopping and eating lunch together. I do like it much better this way.

The silence gets broken when Jaden's suddenly starts, "My girlfriend is also a fan of yours now." I look up from my food.

"Who?" I ask. I am actually confused.

"My girlfriend, Arden," he answers. *Now* it makes sense.

"I didn't know you were together. Well done!" My surprise was evident.

"Thanks," Jaden responds and chuckles.

"The girls really want you to come to Sia and I's party on Friday."

"I don't think that's a good idea," I respond. I can feel fear running through my body, just by the thought of it. I empty my beer to relax.

"You drink a lot, don't you?" Jaden asks, shooting toward me a judgmental look. I hate that look.

"Why do you even care?" I answer.

"I don't," he answers. Silence follows.

"How much do you drink daily?"

"I thought you didn't care," I say, with a smirk. I like that he is curious.

"Is it *that* much?" he asks and looks playfully at me. Oh boy, he should know who he's playing games with.

"I drink a lot, but it doesn't affect me," I finally answer.

"Oh, it doesn't? I would like to see that in person," Jaden continues. He's *so* annoying – I kind of love it.

"Is that a challenge?" I say with a smirk and lean toward him. This is so much fun.

"No, more like an experiment," Jaden says and leans toward me too. We both start laughing out loud. Jaden wants me to come to the party on Friday, and get the experiment rolling. I think I should seriously consider going.

On our way back home, I have the honor of picking the music in the car. I go through my music on Spotify and put on my favorite playlist. At first, he looks surprised, and then he turns up the volume.

We are stuck in traffic. Jaden turns down the music a bit and looks at me. He's about to say something, but his phone rings. He picks it up.

"It's my mom," he tells me and moves the phone up to his ear.

"Yes, he's with me," Jaden says on the phone. He's drumming his fingers on the wheel to the song playing quietly in the background. Why did his mother ask if I'm with him?

"We are on our way home now, but we are stuck in traffic," Jaden ends the conversation and puts the phone down.

"Your mom is fucking worried. She thought you had run off again," he tells me, looking directly at the suddenly moving traffic in front of him. No eye contact this time. I feel bad; I wasn't planning on scaring her.

"Also, we are all eating at your house tonight," he says, turning up the music again. We don't talk for the rest of the journey home. I guess they are all pretty close. I don't mean to hurt anyone, but I'm not used to informing people where I am all the time.

CHAPTER FOUR

A lovely smell wafts in as we enter the kitchen. Pizza and a big bowl of salad are waiting on the kitchen counter. We put down all the things we bought. My mom gets up from the dining table and walks as fast as possible toward me. She is holding me in a hug that seems abnormally long. I don't like the thought of her worrying about me. It's not necessary; I'm *fine*.

Mom looks down at the items. "Wow boys, you must have had a long day at the mall. I can't believe you survived that with your anxiety," she says, looking amazedly at me. I've been hoping she's forgotten about that, but I guess mothers don't.

"It has gotten a lot better," I lie, and she smiles. It's just a little white lie... almost true... or maybe not. But, I don't want her to worry. She goes back to her seat and continues her conversation with Judy and my dad.

"Why did you lie to her? You can't possibly have gotten better," Jaden whispers to me as we help ourselves to some pizza.

"Can't you just mind your own business for once? I'm absolutely fine," I whisper back. This has come out rude – I didn't mean for that. I was about to leave the kitchen when Jaden grasps my arm and drags me close.

"You're not fine," he whispers and looks back at our families, who haven't noticed our argument, luckily. Why do they all think I'm mentally ill? Why can't they understand that I'm just a guy trying to figure everything out? I don't need to be looked after like a little baby.

"I can fix you," he whispers and stares directly into my eyes. He loosens his grip on my arm and goes to sit down at the table.

I look at him during the dinner a couple of times, and I can't stop thinking about *I can fix you*. What does he mean by that? I'm fine... absolutely fine. I'm not mad at him though... not at all. In fact, I think I have a soft spot for him because of his concern for me. I mean... yeah, it can be annoying, but the way he said it made it seem so... err, *mysterious*? This is weird; I don't need to be fixed, but I really want to know how's he planning on fixing me. It's all too much... I need a cigarette. Jaden isn't a fan of smoking. I smoked one before we drove home tonight... he can't stand the smell.

I get up from my chair. Charles asks Dad about the piano in the living room.

"We had it at our old house and couldn't dare to get rid of it," Dad explains. I used to love playing it.

"Olly, can you play the piano?" Charles asks me.

"Umm, I used to play, but I haven't touched a piano in three years," I explain. Everyone's eyes are on me; everyone except Katy and Sam, who are building houses of cards on the floor, and Sia, who isn't here.

"Olly is actually really good at it. He used to play all the time when he was younger," Mom remarks and smiles proudly at me. Charles points to the piano at the end of the room and asks if I want to give a little performance.

"I don't really know. It might sound awful," I try this excuse. The pressure is making me nervous.

"I'm sure it will be fine. Just try," Dad tells me.

I walk over to the piano and sit down. I have missed playing it. I sit down, run my hands over the keys, and press the first one.

I feel like Tom Odell when I play the piano. I can't help but open my mouth slightly. Every sound rushes through my body. I can barely keep my ass on the seat. My curls move, as my head follows my feet stomping on the wooden floor beneath me. No booze or cigarette can replace this feeling. I feel free.

I hit the last note and come to a stop. I'm out of breath. It's funny they're clapping so much. It's making me blush. I can't see Jaden at the table anymore... well, I'm happy. He doesn't have to see my cheeks go all red. I'll ask them though... I want to know where Jaden is. Charles informs me that Jaden has left to pick Sia up from work, but Judy tells him that Sia doesn't get off from work before eleven. I look up at the digital clock on the oven. It's only 7 pm.

I am sitting by the window and smoking my last cigarette tonight with the window opened. I keep replaying the day in my head. It has been *amazing*. Jaden's words keep coming back. *I can fix you.* So simple, yet I can't seem to stop thinking about it.

Mom comes in and sits down on my bed. I can see she has a hard time accepting my smoking habit, so I stub out the cigarette into a plant pot. It's dead already; a small butt won't matter. She looks around the room. I still haven't sorted out all the boxes or the new things from today.

"We can move the piano up here if you want," she offers, with a spark in her eyes.

"That would be nice. I actually enjoyed playing today," I tell her. I'm relieved to say it out loud to someone. She smiles.

A few minutes of silence, and then Mom suddenly says, "Are you planning on going to Sia and Jaden's party on Friday?" How does she even know that I'm invited?

"I don't really know," I tell her and glance toward the dark garden.

"You should go. Then you can make some new friends and stuff." Why does everyone treat me like I'm in some kind of rehab?

"Just consider it at least," she adds and gets up from the bed.

"I will," I sigh. I don't really want to think about this right now. It isn't often that I feel this calm. She walks over to me and kisses my forehead. I can't even remember when I had last gotten a motherly kiss like that.

"Goodnight, sweetie."

On her way out of the room, she asks me if I would like to come with her to work some day and try playing the piano they have in the theater. She seems nervous about asking me, as if she is almost sure I will say no.

"I would love to," I respond, and she leaves my room. Although her back is turned toward me as she is walking out my door, I know she's smiling.

CHAPTER FIVE

I wake up to the sound of my dad's voice. I open my eyes slightly; he is standing at the door and is about to knot his tie.

"Where are you going?" I manage to ask, rubbing the sleep off my eyes.

"To work, Olly. It's Tuesday," he explains and laughs at my confusion. It's Tuesday already? It's weird to see my dad look so damn serious with his suit on. When I was little, he was always the funny dad who wore really old and embarrassing clothes. He actually looks nice now.

"Jaden is standing at the front door, waiting on you. So, get up," he says and walks downstairs. Jaden? Downstairs? Waiting on me? I get up and find the pair of sweatpants I had on yesterday and a big yellow hoodie. The floor is cold, so I put on some socks before heading downstairs.

Jaden is standing outside with a big dog beside him, – a mastiff. My grandparents had one when I was very little. Jaden looks so masculine, with the big dog sitting on his command.

"Do you want to join us on our morning walk?" he asks, while patting the big dog. The sky is pink behind him; the sun is rising. It's the end of spring, so the sun rises very early.

"What's the time?" I ask and yawn loudly. My body is leaning against the door, and my legs feel weak. It's way too early to be out of bed... Why am I not sleeping right now?

"Ten minutes past six," Jaden announces and puts his phone back into his jeans pocket. He's wearing a gray sweater over a black t-shirt, and his hair is a mess.

"You're a crazy person," I complain, and Jaden laughs. He looks so different right now – so down to earth. His eyes look tired, but there's so much cheer in them. Jaden asks me if I'm going to join them.

"You two can just walk without me. I need to change before I can leave the house," I explain. I must admit, it sounds pretty nice.

"Why? you look great, and there's no one out here yet, so no one will see you anyway." Did he just say I look great? I look down the street; it's deserted. Fine. I put on my shoes and jacket and check if there's a pack of cigarettes and a lighter in the pocket. There is. I *need* my morning cigarette.

I leave the house and close the door behind me. Wait... I should tell them before leaving so they don't freak out again and make calls here and there. I open the door again and yell to my dad that I'm leaving, I guess he'll have Mom know.

We start walking down the sidewalk, and now it strikes me that Jaden is actually walking with a mastiff, Buffy, on a leash. I ask him whose dog it is. He tells me that it belongs to an old man living in the neighborhood who can't walk that well anymore. So, Jaden walks it almost every morning and helps him buy groceries sometimes as well. He's so adorable I can barely believe him.

We come by a little coffee shop. How can it be open so early? Jaden asks me if I want a coffee, but I don't have any cash. He insists on paying, and I'm left outside with Buffy alone. The dog breathes heavily and licks my chin as I sit down next to him. He's so calm, unlike the one my grandparents had. Jaden told me that he's quite old. I run my hand down his soft fur. I look around me. The neighborhood is nice and quiet.

Jaden comes out with two drinks in his hands and smiles when he notices me sitting next to Buffy. We walk down the road and turn toward a little path that goes into a close-grown forest. He tells me about his soccer training. I love hearing him speak; his voice relaxes me so much.

"What's your passion?" he asks me and releases Buffy from the leash so that he can walk freely around the trees.

"I love playing piano, I guess," I simply answer. This reminds me of Jaden's sudden disappearance last night. I ask him about it.

"I just needed a bit of fresh air, but the part I did hear was... was phenomenal," Jaden answers and looks nervously at the ground. Why is he suddenly stuttering? What is he hiding?

"If you thought it was *phenomenal*, how could you leave?" I ask, feeling bad for pushing him, but I want answers.

"It's complicated," Jaden answers simply, and I change the subject. He probably just needed a break after *babysitting* me all day.

We leave the forest. I can't recognize the street we are in.

"Where are we?" I question, and he points to the backside of two houses in front of us. Those are ours. I can see the window of my room. Jaden puts the leash on Buffy again and leaves with him. He's going to return Buffy to his owner. I walk home and enter through the back entrance to the garden; Dad is just about to leave for work.

CHAPTER SIX

The smell of alcohol in the room reminds me of the day I'd left the apartment. All that's missing is the strong smell of fresh weed. They don't party like us, which is good because I don't really miss it.

There are people drunk and dancing, singing off key. I'm standing in the open kitchen and looking around the room. Sia and Leah are walking toward me with a bunch of girls I haven't seen before. I manage to ask them, over the loud music, if they had seen Jaden. I feel like talking to him right now. He's apparently out buying more liquor with some of the other guys. The girls want me to join them on the dancefloor. I can't dance, but I go with them anyway, not wanting to stand alone.

I leave the dancefloor, and I'm thirsty. Jaden and the guys from the restaurant the other day walk into the kitchen as well. They place the bottles of liquor they've just bought on the counter. They're soaked from the rain. The water from Jaden's wet hair is dripping down his forehead, and his white t-shirt is now see-through. He looks really hot. I need to stop staring and turn my attention back to the beer in front of me.

"You look awesome," Jaden tells me, and brushes my neck as he walks past me to get some paper cups from a cupboard. I stop myself from answering; I don't trust my ability to speak right now. His eyes sparkle, and his tongue sticks out a little as he reaches for more cups.

"Are you having fun?" he whispers in my ear, and shivers run down my back. Does he know how his behavior affects me right now? I hope there's a hot gay boy in here. I'm not used to going so many days without sex, and I need to get distracted from these sudden strong emotions for Jaden.

"Olly?" A girl shouts in the distance. I look up. *Kayla?* She runs over to me and hugs me tightly. Jaden and the guys leave the kitchen. Kayla was my best friend back in grade school. I have missed her so much since we *broke up*. She didn't like the people I was starting to hang out with back then – like Adam. I chose them instead of her because I thought then that I was doing the right thing. I found the opposite to be true too late.

"Are you okay? I just heard about Meghan's death a few days ago," she asks and lets go of me. A boy walking past us hears her.

"Meghan? Isn't she that slut who got raped?" he asks us harshly. Another guy hears him and laughs even louder. The guy in front of us continues shouting mean things about Meghan like *I would have raped her too if I had had the chance*. This makes me so angry, I want to punch him in the face real bad.

"If you don't shut up right now, I'll kick you in the balls so hard, you won't ever be able to walk again!" I shout and feel tears building up – I want them to. He laughs at me and thrusts me against the counter behind me. Kayla pushes the guy hard in retaliation and shouts that he should leave. He ignores her and keeps his eyes on me.

"If you don't crawl home to your homo friends right now, I will personally kick you back to where you belong, faggot!" he shouts in my face. Jaden and Sia rush out from either side. Jaden grabs and pulls me away out of the kitchen and up the stairs.

Jaden forces me into a room – his own. He pushes me gently down on his bed. I don't want to sit down; I want to go home. Tears are rolling down my cheeks, and I can barely breathe.

"I'm not going to apologize to that idiot, if that's what you want," I manage to tell him through my sobs, gasping for air. He sits down next to me and sighs.

"I'm not going to," he assures me and pulls me into his arms. I can't stop crying. It's the first time since her death that I'm really crying. There are too many emotions, and I can't deal with them all. Gaah! I can't breathe. Minutes pass in silence; The only sound is that of my gasps and sobs. He asks me to take deep breaths, and I try that. I can feel Jaden's heart beating. He now wants to know about Meghan. I know he's trying to make me feel better, but that doesn't matter. It's sweet though.

"She was like a sister to me," I start, and at this point, I just break down. He lets me. I haven't felt this safe in a very long time.

"Hey, sorry for talking snit about her last Saturday. I didn't know her like you did. Sorry," he whispers close to my ear and hugs me tighter.

When did Jaden get so close? His left hand is running up and down my spine, and his right is massaging my thigh. He can't be serious. I'm not crying anymore; my eyes are almost dry, and my wet cheeks are getting warmed up against his warm and soft neck. I can only now hear our heavy breathing. He kisses my hair. My heart is beating like crazy – no longer because of anger, but because of something much stronger. I really want him, but I can't. He brings his hand up from my thigh and places it under my jaw, lifts it a bit, and he kisses my forehead. My eyes look up at his, but they are closed. His hair is still slightly wet from the rain, and his lips are apart. I can see his white teeth. He's beautiful. My thumb strokes his lower lip. His eyes open to reveal his pretty blue eyes. I want him. His head is now as close to mine as possible, but our lips don't touch. He looks at me, and his eyes ask for permission to kiss me. No words are needed; my eyes answer back. My heart is pounding. I don't think my body can handle this much longer... his lips touch mine.

I think I've just stopped breathing. His hand is ruffling my hair. He tastes amazing – a mixture of vodka and pizza. His tongue is begging to explore my mouth – I let it. The kisses get slower and longer. We both want more.

The door suddenly opens. We jump away from each other and look at the opened door. No one walks in. I can hear Kayla's voice; then her head shows up behind the door.

"Oh, there you are!" she shouts and hugs me. She tells me that the boy, whose name is apparently Chris, has left now. Jaden squeezes my shoulder and leaves the room. Kayla doesn't seem to notice how flushed Jaden and I are. I wish she hadn't interrupted us, but in a way, that's good, or it might have gotten too far. It was just a kiss, maybe the best I have ever experienced – but just a kiss nonetheless. Kayla snaps her fingers in front of my face. I'm getting distracted from my thoughts. She laughs at me.

"Did I interrupt something?" she asks, looking confused, as she sits down next to me. I fall backward on the bed and sigh. It feels like the old days when I used to tell her anything and everything. She lies down next to me. I tell her about the kiss. She sits up and slaps me in my face. It warms my cheeks. Why isn't she happy? I've just kissed a really hot boy.

"He's Arden's boyfriend, idiot!" she exclaims and throws herself down next to me again. I totally forgot. I feel bad – why would he kiss me when he's with Arden, and wait, does that mean he's straight? God I'm so stupid. I think I should defend myself.

"*He* kissed me!" I add, but it doesn't help much. I still feel guilty about it. Arden has been so lovely and welcoming, and then, less than a week later, I kiss her boyfriend.

Kayla asks if it was good. I know she feels bad about asking, because we probably shouldn't be talking further about it, but she's curious like she always has been. I describe it for her, and she squeals in excitement. We are *so* cliché, it almost hurts.

We both go downstairs again, after lying on Jaden's bed and catching up on life for an hour or two. We throw ourselves in a couch. I'm trying not to think about what happened, but the places where his lips and hands have touched me still have goosebumps. I need to move on though – he's just another straight boy looking for some fun and experimenting. Ironically, I feel cheated on, when really, it's Arden who should feel that way.

CHAPTER SEVEN

I wake up on the couch in their living room. Some girls are talking and laughing loudly at a distance. My body is heavy; It smells so strongly of sweat and liquor that it makes my eyes water. I get up from the couch; I still have all my clothes on.

"Good morning!" Sia shouts from the kitchen. I walk over to her. The floor is sticky under my bare feet. Where are my socks? Sia, Kayla, and Arden are all sitting around the dining table, eating some breakfast cereal. Kayla pats the free chair next to her. I sit down. Arden asks me if I've slept well, and I nod without knowing clearly if I had even slept. A few boys walk down the stairs and join us. Jaden appears too, but he doesn't sit down. He's looking for a glass in the kitchen.

"Did Adam try to contact you last night?" Kayla asks me. I get my phone out of my back pocket. 7 missed calls and 13 texts from him. Fuck. I still haven't contacted him at all. I let her see it for herself.

"He's crazy" is all she says and shows it to the other girls. I ask her why she wants to know. The girls nervously look up at Jaden. Arden explains that he'd showed up last night. Jaden turns around from the sink and looks at her; the other boys do the same.

"Was Adam on my lot?" he asks angrily. It's like he didn't hear her right.

"Don't even start, Jaden," Sia answers, "he wasn't here to fight you. He was here to talk to Olly." I gulp and ask them what Adam said. Arden explains that he was very drunk and that said I belonged to him and should come back immediately or there was going to be trouble. My heart is beating fast again. Jaden smashes a glass into the sink and breaks it. Arden gets up from her chair and tries to calm him.

"I'm going to make sure that bastard stays away!" Jaden shouts and runs up the stairs again. Arden follows him.

"I'm sorry. I should have stayed in the apartment. Now, I have just taken all my problems and made them yours," I say, feeling guilty. One of the boys, Evan, smiles at me and tells me that I'm one of them now, and that they will protect me. The girls nod. It warms my heart.

"You're a part of the family now," Sia says. I don't get why they're being so nice to me – I've just made Jaden really mad.

"The yellow dress or the white one?" Sia asks me and stands, with both dresses in her hands, only in her underwear. I am lying on the bed in her room and helping her pick an outfit. Both of our families are going out today for brunch and bowling.

"The yellow one. It's very nice," I answer. She puts it on and spins around. She's so beautiful.

"Hey, about the whole *Adam-came-last-night* situation, I just want to apologize for making Jaden pissed. Do you think he will forgive me?" I ask her, and she sits down next to me on the bed.

"Olly, he isn't mad at you; he's protective of you," she responds and smiles at me. Protective about me? This wasn't my impression of his behavior.

Jaden walks into the room. It's obvious that he's avoiding eye contact with me. I still can't believe we actually kissed last night. He tells us that our parents are pretty mad because we aren't dressed yet. She quickly ties her hair into a bun. I still haven't changed yet.

"Olly, you can borrow some clothes from me. Your parents have already locked your house and driven off with our parents, Katy, and Sam," he explains, and I follow him into his room, which is just beside Sia's. I don't feel comfortable being alone with Jaden, not after what's happened in here last night. Please don't bring that up, please don't bring that up. I just really wanna avoid that right now. Jaden lightly throws black skinny jeans and a white hoodie at me and leaves the room without saying anything – it is evident that he doesn't want to be alone with me either. The jeans are a bit too big for my lean thighs; I didn't expect to be of the same size as him – his legs are muscular. I quickly run my hand through my curly hair and dash downstairs.

Sia is standing with my socks and shoes in her hand; she tells me that they found them behind the sofa. Arden is standing beside her. She swallows a pill. The poor girl is feeling quite sick apparently.

The three of us leave the house and join Jaden in his car. Arden is coming with us, even though this is supposed to be a family thing. Kayla told me last night that their relationship is very serious. They have been together for around two years now. Shit.

Sia and Arden are sitting at the back. The girls are choosing the music. It's clearly annoying Jaden, but he doesn't say anything. He draws his attention toward me instead and asks if the rumors are true about how I lost my driver's license. The girls turn down the volume and want to know too.

"What have you heard?" I ask him.

"That you were around ten people in the car, you had all been drinking a lot, and were yelling out of the windows," he tells me, and the girls say that they have heard the same story. I tell them that I can't remember much from that night, even though it was only about a month ago.

"But, is it true?" Sia asks and looks at me like I'm some crazy person. I'm kind of used to that look by now.

"I'm pretty sure we were eight people – not ten – not that it isn't too many for a five-person car. We were all drunk, as you have heard... we had also been smoking some strong herbs that Adam had from a *friend* – not that it makes the situation better at all – but like I told you... I can't really remember much," I tell them, and the girls go speechless. Jaden just chuckles while parking in front of a nice restaurant. Arden follows Sia out of the car. I'm about to get out too when Jaden grabs my arm. His touch is familiar now, leaving the same shivers down my spine as last night's.

"I'm glad you didn't die," he tells me in a low voice and smiles weakly at me before leaving me alone in the car. I never stopped to think then if our actions were life-threatening – but they really were. I quickly get out and run up to the others, who are about to walk into the restaurant. I hate how Jaden can fuck my brain up like that.

A waitress leads us to our parents, Katy, and Sam, who are sitting at a long table. We greet them and take the last four chairs, two on each side at the end of the table. Sia and I are sitting next to each other opposite Jaden and Arden. I look around the restaurant. It is beautiful – chandeliers hanging from the ceiling, wine bottle decorations in the windows, and a dark red vintage-ish carpet on the floor. Sia taps me on the shoulder, and I realize that everyone is walking to the buffet at the end of the room. Jaden turns around and looks at me. I can't understand what emotions he's trying to show here, if he's showing any at all. What does he want from me?

I get an idea as I watch Katy coloring in her book. I borrow one of her pens. Jaden, Sia, and Arden are looking at me with confusion.

"We can play draw and guess," I suggest and wave the white napkin lying next to my plate. Jaden thinks it's a great idea, and the girls just go with the flow. We team up – Jaden and Arden against Sia and I.

The first few rounds were pretty laid-back, but now all four of us are laughing and shouting. I find myself crying with laughter. Our parents ask us to turn down the noise because there are other people in the restaurant as well.

Jaden gets up from his seat; Sam has just told him that there are pancakes in the buffet.

"Do you want one too, Olly?" he asks me, and I nod. Arden acts hurt and puts her hand on her heart.

"Aren't you going to ask your girlfriend?" she teases him, pretending to be in shock. We all laugh. Sia tells her that she should be careful because Jaden might replace her with me. I wish he did.

"Do you want one, babe?" Jaden asks Arden and kisses her on the lips. She says no with his lips still on hers, and he leaves for the buffet. Arden gives him a glance as he walks away – she's so in love. Why did Jaden kiss me? He has the most amazing girlfriend ever.

Jaden comes back with a plate and two forks. He places the plate between us, and we share the pancakes while the game continues. The girls make fun of us as Jaden feeds me with his fork. I know he's just acting, but something about the sparkle in his eyes makes it feel so real.

The bowling alley is almost empty when we arrive. Our parents have gone to the counter to pay. Jaden and Arden are buying drinks and snacks, and Sia and I have taken the kids down with us to pick some bowling balls. I love these people more than I thought I would. It's so weird. I feel like I've known them all my life; I feel calm around them.

The four of us team up in twos – the boys versus the girls. We make a rule that whenever the other team makes a strike, you have to take a shot. Jaden and I agree that I will take his, because he has soccer training tonight and will be the driving us home, and also because I was stupid enough to tell him they *don't affect me.*

Luckily, the girls aren't that good at bowling, so I only had to take a few hits and didn't get drunk. The girls, on the other hand, are very drunk, because Jaden is a psycho at bowling. Of course, he is; he makes a strike every third go or something. I am the absolutely worst one, but that doesn't matter. I still have an amazing time dancing to the music playing in the background. At times, I think about smoking a cigarette, but then I forget all about it. Maybe, I don't need them *all* the time.

A dance song plays loudly in the background, and Jaden starts shuffling – he looks so cool in the blue light. Sam wants to learn how he shuffles, so Jaden tries to teach him. He's really good at it – not Sam, Jaden. Sam still needs a lot of practice. Seeing this, I can only imagine how great a big brother Jaden has been, being there for him while I haven't.

We are driving home. I'm no longer sober. The girls at the back are laughing loudly about something stupid. I lean back and try to ignore it – not the girls – but Jaden's gaze. I can feel him looking at me every second. It's pretty awkward. He is probably debating if he should talk to me or keep quiet. Can't he just open his damn mouth instead of being so mysteriously quiet?

He pulls over in front of their house. He's just going to drop us off before he drives off for soccer training. The girls jump out of the car. I open the door and am about to leave when I feel Jaden's hand grabbing my arm. Does he *always* have to be so fucking dramatic? I turn and look at him.
"You do that quite often, don't you?" I ask and glance at his hand still holding my arm. He loosens his grip. He's nervous and takes a deep breath.
"About the kiss last night – let's just act like it didn't happen. Okay?" he says and looks me directly in my eyes. This idiot – he's trying to be so perfect, but he fucking isn't.
"What have we been doing up until this point?" I ask, annoyed. He is obviously afraid that I'm going to tell Arden.
"I just need to make it clear that no one can know about it. You don't want Adam to figure out about it, do you?"
Wow… now, he's just being an asshole.

"Don't threaten me," I shout back at him, feeling a bit sorry for him, but stowing the emotion away. Jaden asks me to leave his car; he needs to get to soccer training on time. I lean back in the seat to annoy him. He isn't going to control me; I've been controlled enough in my life. Jaden sighs loudly and leans back in his seat too. A few seconds of silence follow, but I can't keep my thoughts inside of me.

"Was kissing me a part of your plan, huh?" I ask and turn my body. I sit and stare at him. He turns his head and looks at me, confused. He asks me what I mean by 'plan'.

"The plan of fixing me," I continue and wait for an answer. He smiles at me. I ask him why he's smiling.

"You remember," he says in a low voice. His eyes are studying me intensely. I really don't get him and his stupid smile. He isn't going to give me any answer... no point talking to him then. I'll leave the car now. I don't need this confusing idiot in my life. Everything is finally working out for me... and then he had to kiss me and mess with my feelings.

CHAPTER EIGHT

The room is crowded with people of all ages. I feel awkward between the many strangers. Katy has been given a lot of presents. It's her 5th birthday today, and around fifty people are here to celebrate. My parents are standing at a distance with Sam. They're greeting some people. I spot Arden, Sia, and Jaden of course, walking in my direction. Jaden's eyes meet mine. He looks away; so do I.

People are finding their assigned seats; they're smiling sweet, but confused, at me. Everyone knows each other, except me. On my way out the door, I walk into a boy my age, kind of hot, and smiling like the rest of them.

"Sorry, Olly," he says. How does he know my name? He read the confusion on my face and tells me that Jaden told him. Of course, he did.

"Where are you going?" he asks me, glancing at the people trying to find their seats.

"Um, I just need some fresh air," I tell him and shrug. He follows me outside and sits down on a bench next to the front door of the local hall. I sit down next to him. He's wearing a nude sweater with a white shirt underneath and a pair of light blue jeans. He looks nice. My mom told me this morning that I looked great, but I'm not sure anymore. My black jeans with holes in the knees, gray t-shirt, and black vintage bomber jacket don't seem to fit in here.

I get my packet of cigarettes and lighter out of my jacket. I light one and enjoy the calm feeling rushing through my body. The boy asks if he could have one too, so I let him take one from the packet. I light it for him and ask him his name.

"Liam," he manages to tell me with the cigarette between his lips. I repeat it. I don't recognize that name.

"Are you from here?" I ask, and he shakes his head. That's probably why he doesn't sound familiar. He explains that he's a friend of the family.

Charles comes out of the door. He tells us that the appetizer will be served in a few minutes. Liam gets up from the bench, stubs out his cigarette on the ground, and smiles at me before walking inside. He seems like a cool guy. I take a few more drags of mine. I feel a little anxious.

"Can you play the birthday song on the piano?" Charles suddenly asks me, and I notice that he hasn't walked in yet.

"Yeah, I think so," I reply. I haven't played it in ages, but it's quite simple. He asks me if I want to play it before we start eating. I hesitate, but nod anyway. My lips are sealed with nervousness, and my stomach knots with nerves. But, I want to play so bad.

He leads me to the piano at the corner of the room, not too far away from the tables. Katy smiles widely at me. I smile back. There is an empty chair next to Jaden; I assume that is where my seat is. I sit nicely at the piano I think and press the first key and start playing on Charles' signal. Many of the guests turn their attention toward me, and they start singing the birthday song for Katy, sitting satisfied on her seat where everyone can see her. She's truly a little princess.

I look up while playing and catch Liam's eyes. He's sitting across from the seat I assume is mine. He smiles; I smile back. But, my smile disappears as I realize that Jaden isn't in his seat. Of course, he isn't. I *knew* he didn't enjoy watching me play. He lied when he said that I sounded *phenomenal*, and I *knew* it. Arden spots the disappointment on my face and sends me a pitiful smile. It's not needed; I'm fine. Why would I care if everyone else seems to enjoy it?

I play the last notes on the piano, and everyone claps — except Jaden, who still isn't here. Katy pushes her chair back and runs over to me, jumps up into my arms, and hugs me tightly around my neck.

"Thanks, Olly," she whispers in my ear, and I put her down on the floor again.

"Of course, sweetie," I tell her, and she runs back to her seat all excited. Jaden is entering the room and sits down on his seat. Arden kisses him on the cheek and asks him something. He just shrugs it off. What's wrong with that boy?

Charles walks over to me and thanks me for playing. I ask him if I may play a few more. I honestly don't want to sit next to Jaden; it will be awkward, and he will probably just get up and leave again. Charles asks if I maybe wanted to eat a bit first. I try to assure him that I'm not hungry, even though I am starving. He lets me play but makes me promise him that I will go eat if I get hungry.

I enjoy this – I truly mean it. Playing for people like this is amazing. Sometimes, people watch me, but then they continue with what they're doing. It's perfect. I don't need their full attention, but it's nice to get some recognition.

I'm taking a break; my fingers are sore. Liam suddenly stands in front of the piano with two glasses of wine. He hands me one, and I thank him.

"You're a great player," he throws me a compliment after taking a sip. My eyes search for Jaden in the room; I want him to see that I can talk to guys other than him as well. Liam seems to realize that I am distracted and places his glass of wine on the piano, probably to get my attention. So, I look up at him.

"Look, Olly, I think you deserve to know – Jaden send me to figure out how you were doing, and if you're feeling alright," he explains to me and looks guilty.

"You must be kidding me!" I exclaim and look around the room. There he is. He's standing far away and is making small talk with an old man – his granddad probably. I thank Liam for the wine and his honesty before getting up.

I walk toward him. I swear I'm so tired of his games. I need to know what's going on. Wait... I have no clue what to say. Shit! Should I just turn around and leave? I don't think he'll spot me. I have to have something... a plan... to say something to him. Damn! It's too late – he's seen me. Why is he giving me a warm smile? What is his deal? Man, he's so confusing!

"Hey, Olly! This is the man whose dog we walked the other morning, remember?" I nod slowly, shocked by his kindness. I greet the old man, Richard. I inhale some much-needed air and try to put my annoyed face on. He can't just act like nothing's happened. It might be stupid... I mean, he just wanted know how I was doing. Why did he have to send his friend for that? He could've done that himself.

Richard walks away, and Jaden turns to me, leaning against the wall beside him with a big smirk on his face.

"Do you want to go somewhere... private?" he asks, and I sigh at his confidence.

To be honest, I don't even know what I'm doing right now. I'm just following Jaden to a staff bathroom down a long hall. He holds the door open for me – what a gentleman – I think sarcastically and roll my eyes. The bathroom stinks, but I ignore it. He closes the door behind me, walks past me, and leans against a wall. I don't move.

"So... Did you want to talk?" he asks. Did I *ever* tell him that I wanted to talk? I don't think I did.

"You came over, I thought you wanted to talk. Was I wrong?" he continues, with a teasing smile at the corner of his mouth. He is playing confused – stupid. I walk over to the sink on the wall opposite to Jaden. I still haven't figured out what to say completely.

"There's something I don't understand," I start. As I wash my hands, he looks up from the floor, and our eyes meet in the mirror in front of me.

"If I play so phenomenal, why don't you stay and listen to it then?" I blurt out, really wanting to know. He groans and looks away. I dry my hands with the thin paper and run it over the sink so that it isn't wet – a stupid habit. He closes his eyes and puts his hands in his hair.

"I feel things for you – things that I shouldn't feel because I have a girlfriend. When you play... you get so damn attractive, and I... You just keep messing with my head!" he breathes out, and my eyes widen in surprise.

"Do I mess with *your* head? *You* were the one who kissed me!" I protest and turn around.

"Because, I couldn't keep myself off you anymore!" he shouts back, and it echoes in the bathroom. He walks closer so that our noses almost touch. We're both breathing heavily, and my heart is beating so fast. His blue eyes are staring into my green ones. I grab one of his hands. It's shaking slightly. I give it a soft squeeze before bringing it up to my chest to let him feel how fast my heart is beating to have him near me. I didn't know he felt that way about me.

He smiles insecurely at me, grabs my other hand, and brings it up to his heart. It is beating like crazy too. We stand like this for I don't know how long... just analyzing each other's faces – his small ears, his beautiful, clear eyes, and thin lips. I want it all. He leans in and bites my lower lip. The butterflies in my stomach go crazy. We start making out. He takes my hands above my head until they rest against the cold mirror behind me. My body shivers – and I let out a moan – as he suddenly lifts me up on the sink. He leaves kisses down my neck and squeezes my thighs with his warm hands. My eyes are closed, and I'm silent – only a few moans escape my lips. I bring my hands down around his neck. His muscles tighten as my cold hands brush against his warm skin. His hands move up from my thighs and take off my jacket. We kiss deeply, and his hands slide up under my t-shirt. He's about to take it off me. I can't wait.

Is this his phone ringing? *Why now?* He groans loudly and leaves a kiss on my lips, before answering the phone. His finger is drawing circles on one of my thighs as he talks. I just want him to finish the call so that we can continue from where we left off.

"Okay, we'll come back now," he tells the person on the other end and hangs up. *What?* He kisses me softly on my lips and tells me that his dad called and told that they have started to eat and Katy doesn't know where we are. I put on my jacket and jump down from the sink. We can't ruin her birthday like we unintentionally did with Sam's.

We're standing behind the door of the big room and can easily hear people talking and laughing. I reach for the door handle, but Jaden removes my hand.

"Can we do this again someday?" he asks and looks shyly at the ground between our feet. He's so cute.

"Of course. But, when? I don't think I can wait for too long." He looks up in relief and gives me a short smile. Then, it seems that he looks kind of sad.

"I'm afraid you'd have to wait for a bit, because I'm going to stay over at Arden's for a few days. After that, we're leaving for the summer cottage, where we can be together all the time, without any girlfriend or Adam." He tells me and runs one of his hands through my small curls. I was told about the summer cottage only yesterday. Apparently, like a tradition, Sia and Jaden's family leave for their cottage for a whole week in the summer. In the last two years, my family has been joining them.

"I can wait for a few days," I tell him and plant a quick kiss on his cheek. He cups my face and brings our lips together for a few seconds before we head inside, join the others at the buffet, and make plans for the trip. It's going to be absolutely amazing.

PART 2
-
SUMMER

CHAPTER NINE

The yellow fields seem to keep going on, on both sides – where's this summer cottage? I keep my eyes on the view from the backseat of the car. It's beautiful here in the morning; I actually wouldn't mind waking up at 6 am another time to take in this beauty.

I've spent the last few days packing and renovating my room with help from my dad after he would come home from work. It was nice to do something together, even though we didn't really talk much.

I turn up the music a bit more, ignoring that it's above the recommended volume for your ears. It's necessary right now because Sam and his friend are talking loudly about a video game next to me. Sam's got permission to bring a friend to the cottage so that he's not bored through the next week. Mom turns in the passenger seat and offers us a chocolate biscuit each. I take one and ask her when we'll be reaching.

"At 9 am," she informs me and turns her attention back to the book lying on her lap. I check the time on my phone – there's still an hour to go.

I hear the sound of car doors closing and open my eyes slightly. I'm sitting alone in the car. The others are standing outside greeting Judy, Charles, and Katy – but where's Jaden and Sia? I open the door and climb out. My dad is starting to empty the car. I stretch my body and yawn louder than I'd expected.

"Hey, Sleeping Beauty!" a guy whispers behind me. Jaden. I turn around, and I'm dragged into a quick hug. He looks great. Everyone else is getting inside the big cottage. It's beautiful, all made out of dark brown wood in the clearing of a dense forest.

"Do you like it?" Jaden asks and chuckles at my seemingly funny expression. I blush slightly and shut the car door behind me.

"It's massive," I reply and Jaden laughs at my numbness, grabs my arm, and drags me inside. There's an open kitchen to my right, where our parents are standing, a big lounge area with a fireplace to my left and a long dining table standing at the end of the room, with a little corridor after it. The floor and walls are all made of wood. Jaden gives me a few seconds to get a good look at the big open room, before taking me upstairs with my suitcase. I offer taking it myself, but he insists on carrying it for me.

There are two doors upstairs – a room for Sam and his friend and a room for Sia, Jaden, and me. Katy will be sleeping downstairs in her parents' bedroom.

Jaden opens the door for me; Sia is already sitting on the one-person bed with her bags, so Jaden and I are going to share the double bed, which isn't at all a problem for me – it's actually the perfect arrangement. I greet her and walk over to the big window behind the double bed. There's a beautiful view of a vast clear lake less than a hundred meters away. There are long, shabby, yellow curtains hanging on each side of the window, and the walls are a dark shade of red. It's so nice – reminds me a bit of my room at home, actually.

"Do you want to go down for a swim before lunch?" Jaden asks, standing with his swimming trunks already in his hand. I nod and get mine too. I can't wait to be alone with him. We take turns changing in the bathroom and walk down the little path to the lake, after arranging that the rest of them will come down after unpacking their stuff.

Jaden throws his towel on the grass and runs out on the long lake pier; I do the same. He stands on the very end and jumps into the clear blue water, disappears for a moment, and then he floats up with his hair all wet. I bite my lip – he looks incredible, much like how he looked the night we kissed for the first time.

"Come on beautiful, now it's your turn," he shouts and splashes some water up on me. Luckily, it only touches my toes – it's ice cold, though. How can he stand with his shoulders immersed in the water? I sit down on the edge of the pier and stick my feet under before quickly pulling them up again.

"I can't, it's too cold," I tell him, and he laughs sweetly at me. He swims over to me and puts his cold and wet hands on my thighs, which gives me goosebumps down my whole body. I squeal as he lifts me close to his body and pulls me under the water. I hug him tight, not wanting to get my chest and shoulders underneath too.

"You look so damn cute right know," Jaden whispers into my neck, he can't not know the effect it has on me. He slowly brings the rest of my body under and smirks at my groans. I sweep his wet hair away from his forehead and kiss the spot. My shoulders are under too, and my whole body feels light. I feel his hands under the water – they grip my hips and pulls me even closer to him. Our foreheads touch.

Now I see why he wanted us to get down here behind the bridge – we can finally be together without worrying about someone seeing us. He leans in and bites my lower lip – the beginning of long and deep kisses. My hands tug his hair, and he lifts me up so that our upper bodies are again glued together.

He releases me from his firm embrace when we hear our dads' voices at a distance. I lean in and peck his lips quickly before we both swim away from behind the pier and wave at the rest. They are about to get into the water too. No more privacy for now.

After being in the lake for a few hours, everyone is very worn out, and we decide to walk back to the cottage to grab some lunch before making the bonfire for tonight.

Jaden, Sia, and I are sitting at the end of the table, talking to each other. I take a bite of my sandwich. Jaden opens a beer for himself and offers me one too. I nod, but my mom doesn't seem to agree.

"Olly, do you need to drink *every* day?" she asks and raises an eyebrow at me from the other end of the table.

"I don't drink *every* day, Mom," I tell her in an annoyed tone. Can't she just mind her own damn business? I don't need her to keep an eye on me all the time.

"You could at least take a break while we're here," she states. I feel so angry.

"I don't have an alcohol problem!" I shout. The room is now quiet.

"Then, why do you drink all the time?" she questions in a calm, motherly voice, which makes me even angrier. This is embarrassing.

"Why are you attacking me like this? It's stupid. I haven't said anything to upset you!" I defend myself and run upstairs. I have lost my appetite.

I throw myself on the double bed and close my eyes. A million thoughts are cramming my mind. What's her problem? She has been so nice to me ever since I moved back in. I have done my best to keep a distance so that we don't argue about something stupid like this.

"Sleeping Beauty, wake up" I hear Jaden whisper. He tugs my arm gently. I groan in protest but smile shyly over my new nickname. Why is he so nice to me? I turn around and look up at him sitting next to me on the bed.

"How long have I been sleeping?" I ask, sitting up to stretch. He runs a hand through my curly hair and bites his lip. His eyes are sparkling in the sun coming through the narrow gap between the curtains.

"It's half past three. So, not for that long. The others are at the lake, building the bonfire. I told them that we would come too," he replies. I yawn and nod. It sounds good. I just hope Mom is in a better mood now; I don't want this whole trip to get ruined because of one stupid argument.

"Your pretty little brain is thinking quite a lot, huh?" he asks, pushing me back down and crawling on top of me. I must have zoned out. I put my hands around his neck, and he kisses mine. I wish we didn't have to hide our feelings for each other, but I guess that's just how it has to be. He finds a tender spot and has now started sucking on it; I let out quiet moans next to his ear.

"Careful, you don't want to leave a mark," I caution him through gasps and moans. He pulls away, plants a simple kiss on my nose, and strokes my nose ring with his thumb. I join our lips for another kiss.

"We should probably join the others, so they don't get suspicious," he suggests and pulls me out of the bed with him. I chuckle and follow him downstairs and outside. The sun is shining directly on us as we leave the cottage and walk down the little path to the lake.

Jaden is playing soccer with the boys, and I am looking for branches with Katy and Sia in the bushes below the tall trees. We drop the branches off in a pile beside the bonfire spot that our dads have already prepared with some stones.

"You finally decided to get up," Mom remarks from a distance, visibly pissed. She's sitting on an old bench with Judy. I roll my eyes at her. Is she being serious right now? I ignore her and sit down next to Sia and Katy on the grass. Katy hands me her hairbrush and asks me to brush her hair. I move closer to her and run the wooden brush through her long hair.

This reminds me of the old days – I used to fix Meghan's hair for her dates once a week... well, those weren't really dates... but more like... appointments... in that derelict flat in town. I never really gave much thought to it at first. I mean, come on... she was so sweet. Of course, all the boys in town and outside would kill to date her. Then, there was her day job behind the pub. I don't want to think about her in those situations right now. She was more than just a prostitute – she was like a sister to me.

"Olly, I think her hair is brushed enough now," Sia tells me and puts her hand on my shoulder. I look around and recognize that I'm still sitting on the grass beside the big lake. I must have zoned out again.

"Sorry," I excuse myself and lay the brush down. I move away so that Sia can braid Katy's hair.

"That's alright. What were you thinking about?" she asks me out of curiosity, with a warm smile. I wonder if I should say it; I don't want to ruin the mood, but on the other hand, she did ask herself, and I actually really want to tell her.

"Meghan," I answer, pulling up a straw of grass from the dry ground and twirling it between my fingers. Katy slightly lifts her head.

"Meghan? I saw a picture of a girl in the paper; she was raped. Her name was Meghan too. She was pretty," the little girl tells us and looks dreamily down at the grass in front of her small bare feet. Sia and I look at each other, not knowing what to say next; we, of course, both know that it's the same Meghan, but should Katy know that? Sia nods to give me permission to tell her.

"Katy," I begin, and she turns her head to look at me. I clear my throat and tuck a tress of her hair hanging over one of her blue eyes behind her ear.

"The pretty girl you read about in the paper was actually a good friend of mine before she died," I tell her. She looks at me, confused.

"Do you miss her sometimes?" she asks carefully, staring at me and waiting for an answer.

"Every day," she gets up and hugs me, which makes the braid that Sia just made loosen and fall open. Sia doesn't seem to mind though; she smiles lovingly at her little sister's action and starts over as soon as she sits down in front of her again. My heart sinks at the thought of Meghan – I wish she could be here with me.

CHAPTER TEN

The flames dance around as a light breeze touches them.

I'm sitting between the twins and sharing a twist bread with Jaden. We're both still full after dinner, so we decided to share one.

"Oh fuck, it's hot!" I shout as I pull the bread off the stick. Now, Jaden won't stop laughing at my reaction. He takes the bread out of my hand to stop the pain and puts it on his lap instead. My mom gives me a steely look and tells me to stop cursing. I ignore her – why is she in such a bad mood?

The others decide to go back to the cottage and catch some sleep because tomorrow they're going to a market that's an hour away. Jaden and I are going to stay home – not that my mom was cool about it though – but luckily, my dad thinks it's good that Jaden and I are hanging out more.

"Don't stay out here all night... and be careful not to wake Sia and the boys up when you come inside, okay?" Charles tells us, holding his finger up, pretending to be all serious when we all know that he's just fooling around.

"We won't," I shout back at him, and he laughs, turning around and walking up to the rest.

We're sitting in silence for a few minutes, just staring at the flames and taking some sips of our beers. Jaden rests his head on my shoulder and closes his eyes. We're both already a few cans down.

"When did you figure you're gay?" he suddenly asks, looking up at me. I put my hand in his, stroking it with my thumb. I didn't expect him to want to have this deep conversation right now, being all drunk.

"Um, are you sure you want to hear the story? It's pretty boring," I tell him and run my free hand through his hair.

"Olly, listen," he sits up straight and turns his body so our faces are inches apart.

"I'm scared... I'm fucking scared. Every time you look at me with those pretty green eyes, my heart immediately starts beating like those loud drums they play before the match... and I have never felt something like this before," he tells me and leaves me speechless. I cup his head in my hands and stare into his eyes, which are now watering. Our cheeks press against each other's – so soft and warm.

"I love you," I whisper in his ear. It feels amazing to say this out loud. He pulls back, so our lips are touching again – my nose against his, deep intense kisses, hands under shirts. Jaden gently pushes me down on the cold grass and pulls off my shirt; I pull off his. He lets his hands run down my chest and stomach, before leaving kisses on my neck all the way up to my ear where he nibbles my earlobe. This makes me moan lightly – I'm trying not to be loud.

"Do you want to continue this in the double bed or is here fine?" he asks and gently bites my lower lip.

"We can't do this on the bed. Sia is in the same room," I remind him and put my hands around his neck.

"Sia knows about us," he tells me, leaning in to kiss me, but I push him away.

"She what? How can you be this calm? What if she tells Arden or Adam?" I shout out, sitting up in frustration. Is this a joke to him? He grabs my hands and moves even closer to me. My heart starts beating fast.

"I can be this calm because it's Sia, and she will not say anything to anyone – not even her best friend. So, please relax," he begs me, staring right into my eyes. I breathe in and glance around us. The lake is so quiet, and everything seems so deserted and calm. I breathe in the fresh air. *It's Sia, one of the kindest people I have ever met*, I tell myself and look back at Jaden, who is impatiently waiting for my reaction.

"So, she knows that you are gay or bi or whatever?" I ask, tightening my grip around his hands.

"Sia knows everything, Olly." I look at him in confusion.

"She knew that I was gay before I did, and she knew that I liked you before I did," he explains and runs his hand down my cheek. I love his touch.

"Okay," I answer simply and lie down on the grass again – enough talking for now. Jaden smirks at me before putting his knee on each side of my hips and lying down. Our lips meet.

"You're so fucking handsome," he states against my lips. His hands lift me up by my thighs, making me sit on his back with my arms around his neck. He lets me piggyback, and it makes me squeal. He's so strong – he walks up the path toward the cottage with my weight on him. I kiss him down his neck and run my hands through his soft, cold hair.

"If I'm too heavy just tell me," I say, feeling a bit insecure about my weight, even though I know I'm actually very skinny. He laughs and gives me a quick kiss on my left cheek.

"You're perfect. Don't worry about it." We get to the front door, and I loosen my grip around him so we can go inside, but Jaden doesn't let me.

"What do you think you're doing, babe?" he questions in a muffled voice and tightens his grip around my thighs. Is this even real? I don't answer, just let him carry me in, up the squeaking stairs, and inside the dark room lit only by the moon shimmering through the yellow curtains. Sia snores peacefully as Jaden puts me down on the bed. I suddenly realize that both our shirts are still lying outside and smile instantly. Jaden notices it and looks at me curiously.

"What are you thinking about?" he whispers with a smirk across his face and pushes me gently down on the bed. He crawls on top of me. My body sinks down in the soft duvet.

"You," I whisper back, unbuttoning his skinny jeans slowly before pulling them down as far as I can. He gets up from the bed and pulls them off completely, almost loses his balance but holds on to the bed. I giggle at his clumsiness. He jumps on top of me again, wearing only his briefs, which makes the whole bed move slightly. My hands stroke his bare thighs. I can feel goosebumps forming at my touch. He pulls off my sweatpants and kisses my bare legs in the process. I've never tried being loved like this before. He lets my sweatpants fall on the floor and meets my lips – his blue eyes full of desire.

"It's pretty cold. Can we get under the duvets?" he asks and leaves a soft kiss on my nose which makes my nose ring move a bit. I nod, feeling the draught from the window. Jaden drags me off the bed gently and lays out both the duvets – his and mine – at the foot of the bed. I lie down, and he does so too swiftly, before pulling the duvets over us. A few seconds is all it takes for him to get on top of me again. Our hands and lips freely explore everywhere, and it feels absolutely amazing.

I've had lots of sex over the years, but nothing can be compared to the almost innocent touching we're doing right now.

Minutes later, we are lying on our sides, my leg wrapped around his waist, lips sealed in deep kisses. We both pull away to breathe. I fall on my back and listen to our heavy breathing – it sounds like we had just run a marathon. I turn my head to look at him; his eyes are already on me. We both smile like silly kids and then drift off, sleeping in each other's arms. I'm so in love with this guy.

CHAPTER ELEVEN

I wake up feeling warm and in peace. My head hurts a little as I sit up on the bed and look around – Jaden and Sia aren't in the room. I remember the market. Did Jaden decide to join them anyway? I wonder and lie down again. I remember last night clearly, even though I had been drinking quite a lot. I was excited to spend the day alone with him and hopefully carry on from where we left off. Although, it's cool if he wants to have some family time instead. I pull the curtains to the side and feel the sunlight warm my face. I push Jaden's duvet off me and notice that mine is lying on the floor.

I walk out of the room in only my briefs. The floor is colder out here. There's music playing softly downstairs. *What?* I hurry down the stairs and can't stop myself from smiling widely when I see Jaden, only in briefs too, standing in the kitchen – cooking. What a cliché. A little radio stands on the kitchen counter, playing some pop music I can't recognize.

"Hey!" I say weakly, leaning my elbows on the kitchen island and cupping my head in my palms. He almost jumps in shock, which makes me giggle loudly. He turns around, looking numb because of the shock, but his face softens after a few seconds.

"Are you hungry?" he asks with a smile and starts stirring the scrambled eggs. I walk around the island and hug him from behind.

"Very," I reply, kissing the back of his neck. He mumbles something I can't hear and chuckles.

As he puts down the plates on the little porch table, it smells lovely of bacon and toast. The view of the lake is beautiful and nothing like home. Jaden walks inside again to get the drinks. I look down at the plate in front of me and bring back to mind that time he made breakfast to me at their family café. It looks so delicious. Jaden comes back with two huge glasses of juice and sits down at the table.

We are eating in silence for a few minutes and glancing up at each other now and then. I love the silence – it isn't awkward; it's relaxing.

"Do you want to tell me how you found out you were gay now?" he asks softly and bites his lower lip, probably scared that I don't want to tell him like last night. I smile to assure him that there is nothing wrong with the question. I get why he wants to know; it's confusing to go through.

"It all started when I was at summer camp. I was 12 years old. We were playing some stupid game... I can't remember what it was... and a boy around my age kissed me... and I liked it. I was so scared, and when I came home from camp, I told Kayla. She promised not to tell anyone, but that same night my parents came into my room and had the whole we-will-still-love-you-if-you're-gay talk with me. So, she had told her parents and then they had told mine. I began crying and came out to them, even though I didn't really know it was the thing to do. I came out to my friends two years later. They didn't want to be my friends anymore after that and told the rest of my school. I was bullied for the next few years, but then I met Adam and his friends who accepted me the way I was." I don't like talking about it. I keep my eyes on the food as I speak. Suddenly, I feel Jaden's warm fingers under my chin. He lifts my head slightly, and I look up and meet his eyes.

"You were and still are so brave," he whispers and strokes my chin with his thumb. We sit like this for a few minutes, just staring into each other eyes, but then Jaden pulls his hand away.

"We should probably eat the food before it gets completely cold," he speaks and laughs. We are *such* a cliché, and I love it.

We are standing in the kitchen, cleaning the dishes and talking. He's so beautiful – when he smiles his eyes light up, and I can't help but wonder what I've done to deserve his company.

"You're my dream husband," I state. My eyes widen when I realize what I just said. I hide my slightly blushing cheeks in the kitchen towel – I'm not used to saying stuff like that. He chuckles and brings me close for a tight warm hug. We both haven't put our clothes on yet, but it isn't cold. Jaden throws the kitchen towel away, but I just hide my face against his neck instead. I hate it when I blush. Jaden lifts me up on the counter and gently moves a curl from my forehead before resting his against mine. I can feel his eyes staring at me. I look down at his lips; I want to kiss him so badly, but before I can do anything, his lips are pressed against mine. My stomach twinges, and I feel powerless in his touch.

I am carried to the couch, and we lie down and cuddle. I can't recall a time when I was this carefree. I don't want to go home in a week; can't I just stay here for the rest of my life, waking up to delicious breakfast and a hot guy? I relax within his strong arms and close my eyes.

"Olly, don't fall asleep. I have something to show you," he whispers in my ear, and his warm breath caresses my neck.

"What?" I ask, curiously.

"I will take you there, but we have to put on some clothes first," he explains and makes me feel excited. I turn my head and peck his lips before jumping up from the couch. Jaden laughs at my sudden energy and follows me upstairs.

We take turns showering in the little bathroom in our room. Jaden starts first because he has some preparation to do before his surprise.

I get out of the shower after standing against the cold tiled wall, lost in my thoughts for a few minutes. I can't believe I still haven't broken up with Adam; I wish he could just forget about me completely. And, what about school? I haven't been studying for the last year... and what am I going to do after summer? I can't just sit at home all day.

I don't want to stress over those things right now. I dry my body and put on some fresh clothes – it's nice to be clean after swimming yesterday and not showering after it. My hair is a mess. I try to fix it as I run down the stairs. Jaden is standing again in the kitchen; he's putting some stuff inside a big fabric bag. Picnic? Are we going on a date? He turns around and smiles at me.

"Are you ready?" he asks and lifts the bag down from the counter. I nod and put on my black sneakers; they look great with my blue mom jeans and yellow graphic t-shirt.

We walk down a path, not the one that leads to the lake, but directly into the deep forest. The birds chirp, and Jaden leads the way with the cloth bag in one hand and my hand in the other. I take a good look at his outfit as we walk. His shoes are white converse; he's wearing a dark green long-sleeved t-shirt and black shorts. He looks so good.

"Are we there yet?" I whine, after walking for what feels like ages. I didn't expect the forest to be this deep. Jaden stops walking and turns around to look at me.

"Close your eyes," he instructs and comes around me to cover my eyes with his hands.

After walking this way for a bit, Jaden asks me to stop, his hands still covering my eyes.

"Are you ready?" he asks, kissing me on the back of my head. I nod in excitement. What is it?

"I hope you won't get disappointed," he says before removing his hands. A big beautiful tree house in an old, strong tree like the ones in fairytales is in front of us. I glance at Jaden, who's standing next to me with a wide grin on his lips. He grabs my hand and drags me over to the ladder. I climb up without asking.

As my head pops into the treehouse, my eyes light up. There's a big mattress in the corner and a few bottles of wine on the floor. I look down at Jaden standing at the foot of the ladder, staring at me and biting his lip the way that drives me quite mad.

"Crawl inside," he tells me, and I do so. I sit down on the mattress and take my shoes off. It's pretty dark in here; there are no windows. Jaden crawls inside too and brushes his lips against mine, then going for my left cheek. What a *tease*. He takes his shoes off too and pushes a button on the wall. I look up and see the fairy lights getting switched on around the ceiling. Jaden opens one of the bottles and takes out two wine glasses from the cloth bag. He pours some into a glass and hands it to me. I look around. The whole treehouse is made of the same wood.

"Did you expect more?" he asks shyly, taking a sip of his wine. I pat the space beside me on the mattress, gesturing him to come and sit down next to me. He does.

"I love it. It's very romantic" I whisper, resting my head on his shoulder. He rests his head against mine and wraps his arm around my waist, pulling me closer.

"We bought the summer cottage when I was around thirteen years old. I remember finding this tree house the very first week we were here. I thought the others didn't know about it, so it felt special – this was my secret. As a twin, it's hard to be *you* sometimes, so when I found this place, I got so excited. That day, I took pillows and magazines with me out here. I would tell my parents and Sia that I was playing in the forest, but really I was lying in here thinking," he tells me, and I can feel his body slowly relaxing against mine.

"What would you think about?" I ask out of curiosity. He stares sternly at the ground before looking up at me with a tiny smile on his face.

"Boys, mostly," he says and chuckles without escaping our gaze. I manage to nod slowly, but my mind goes numb. I'm caught in his intense stare. He loosens his grip around my waist and lies down on his back. I lie down next to him, not liking the distance and close my eyes. I know it is stupid but I feel if I close my eyes, I can in some way lock this moment – the space and time, all of it.

"I'm breaking up with Arden when we are back home," he suddenly blurts out. *What?* Is he telling this to me or is he telling himself? They've been together for so long... it must be hard. Well, I know it's because of me. I turn to look at his face – his eyes are closed. He's in the biggest fight of his life – the fight to be himself. Man, I know what it's like; I've been there myself, and it's not nice. I cuddle into his side, and he quickly wraps his arms around me. I wish I had met a guy like Jaden back then.

It's been a few moments and we are lying like this. There's total silence. Adam.

"If you break up with Arden, I will break up with Adam," I hear myself promising him. His eyes open, and he looks at me. Why is there anger in his eyes?

He removes his arms from around me and sits up on the edge of the mattress. Why is he mad? I sit up but keep my distance. I want to give him some space. Is he mad because I mentioned Adam? He gets up from the bed and stands up for a moment. Then, he turns around.

"I don't think you should break up with him in person, though," he tells me and crawls back in.

"I need to," I tell him firmly, but he shakes his head in disagreement. He doesn't even know Adam, so why is he interfering in my relationship with him?

"Can I at least be there? I can just hide behind something," he asks me, running his fingers through my hair. I shake my head and ask him why.

"Because I want to help you if he gets aggressive," he answers in a low tone and runs his fingers along my jawline. *If he gets aggressive?* He is violent against others, not me... He will definitely try to make me come back to him, but not physically hurt me or anything. Ugh! It's annoying...Why can't Jaden trust that I know what I'm doing? I'm not interfering with how he plans to break up with Arden. I'm about to crawl down from the mattress, but his hand grabs mine.

"Please don't leave," he gently begs, keeping his eyes on our hands. His fingers gently slide into the spaces between mine, and he keeps them there. I lean in to kiss him. I don't want to think about Adam anymore for today; I know Jaden just wants to keep me safe.

"I have lunch in the bag if you're hungry," he tells me, kissing my forehead. I nod. We're lying on the mattress, cuddling and talking. Jaden's apparently starting soccer school when summer ends. Of course, he is. I love that he's so passionate about something. He's deep. I wish I were too. "I'm actually pretty hungry," I tell him. He gets the cloth bag standing on the floor, opens it, and hands me a little box with leftovers from the dinner last night. He got one for himself too and two forks. I can't stop myself from smiling – he's too cute. He hands me a fork and looks nervous.

I open my box and look up to see him staring at me. "I hope I didn't set this up to be too big a deal," he asks me. I have already told him that I love it; he shouldn't be nervous. I put down my food and sigh.

"For god sake, Jaden, listen... I just want to be with you. I have never been the one for fancy stuff. But this... this actually feels good. Perfect, even," I tell him, waiting for that beautiful smile that appears on his face. He chuckles, before crawling closer to me with his food.

"You look cute when you put me in my place," he whispers against my lips and then, the next few hours I spent discovering him as he discovers me.

CHAPTER TWELVE

The next morning, we're all sitting around the big dining table; Sia is telling me about this attractive guy she saw at the market yesterday. Jaden is rolling his eyes at her, which makes me laugh. Katy is drawing in her coloring book like her life depended on it. Sam and his friend have already finished eating and are putting their shoes on to head down to the lake.

"Olly, Jaden, did you two have a good time yesterday?" my dad asks, smiling excitedly at us. We both nod, and I tell him about how I got spoiled with good food all day. It makes him chuckle.

"So, you are eating normally again?" he asks, and I nod when it actually hits me that I've not only been eating a lot but that I also haven't had anxiety attacks at any point in this trip. It must be because of Jaden; maybe, he has fixed me without me noticing anything. My mom tells me that she thinks I should have come to the market because there were a lot of cool things. She seems a bit annoyed that I didn't hang out with them yesterday, but I ignore it. I glance over at Jaden sharing cooking advice with my dad. Dad asks him why he isn't studying cookery after summer. Jaden explains to him that he would rather become a professional soccer player and then work at the family café as a side thing because it's more of a hobby for him. He has got so many opportunities because he knows what he's good at; I can't help but feel even more lost. What am *I* good at?

Jaden and I are sitting on the lake pier, talking about random things, when suddenly, a familiar voice comes from behind us. We both turn around and see the beautiful brown-haired girl standing with a red crop top and light denim shorts on. Arden.

"Hey, babe!" Jaden shouts, surprised but happy. He jumps up and holds her in a tight hug. I know that he cares for her, even though it isn't real love. She smiles at me widely, and I get up too.

"You look good," I say, before hugging her. She pulls away and gives me the elevator eyes.

"You too," she tells me genuinely. How can she be this perfect and sweet? I feel bad for Jaden – how is he ever going to break up with her?

"What are you doing here?" Jaden asks and gives her a light kiss. She kisses him back – she's definitely more into it then Jaden.

"Your mom invited me so that I could surprise you," she explains as they walk towards the cottage, leaving me standing on the pier by myself. I guess I have to prepare for third-wheeling the rest of this week. Amazing.

CHAPTER THIRTEEN

I am sitting on blankets, next to a sleeping Katy, with the lake in view. We were in the water for a few hours and have been braiding flower bracelets. It was nice, but I hope I'm not going to be babysitting her for the rest of the week just because Arden's arrived. I haven't seen either her or Jaden since she came. Sia is making lunch with our moms while our dads walk along the lake talking.

"Hey, Olly," my mom whispers, coming close so she can avoid waking Katy up.

"What's up?" I ask and notice a genuine smile across her face. She asks me if I want to go for a walk with her after lunch. A *walk*? I hesitate but nod to agree.

"Great," she replies and walks back again. A *walk*? Is it *only* me and her then? My heart stops when I remind myself of her mood lately. Is she going to have a serious talk with me? I'm a bit scared, but I push it away – there's really no need to worry. Katy wakes up slowly, and we walk back together. I feel like taking a shower. My body feels gross after being in the water for so long.

The water is warm. It feels like my body is boiling against the cold tiles behind me. I wish Judy never invited Arden… I could have him for myself right now… we could probably make out against the wall in our room…

even fight for fun, just to touch each other... *unintentionally*, of course. Wait! Where's she going to sleep? Where am *I* going to sleep? The couch downstairs? Would they really do that? I mean... I'm the *new one* here and mom isn't really a big fan of me right now.

I get out of the shower. The little window is open so that the steam can escape. I dry myself with a towel when I suddenly hear a voice.

"Do you want to go for a walk in the forest before dinner?" says a girl who I now recognize as Arden. Is Jaden there too?

"I actually really want to hang out with Olly. Can we do it later maybe?" Jaden answers. God, I could listen to his voice all day. I lean against the sink, and a smile escapes me. I've missed him so much, and it has only been a couple of hours.

"How is he?" Arden asks softly. I probably shouldn't be listening to this conversation about myself.

"Great, I think. Why?" he replies. I'm more than great, actually.

"I don't know, I'm just so happy that you two are becoming friends. I think he needs a friend like you right now," she tells him, and I feel warm inside. Normally, I would hate that she feels pity for me, but it's actually sweet of her. Why does she have to be so perfect? There's silence for a few seconds, but then Arden continues,

"I understand if you want some alone time with Olly, so I'll just drive into town with Sia tonight." I smile widely, but it fades slightly when I hear the sound of them making out. Jealousy.

"You're the best girlfriend on this planet," he tells her between kisses, and she leaves the room. Shall I hide in here or let him know that I was listening? Before I can reach a decision, the bathroom door opens. His eyes meet mine through the mirror, which makes him jump. I walk over to him, only wearing a towel around my waist. He closes the door behind him.

"I hadn't expected to see you in here," he says with a smirk, glancing down at my skinny torso. I wish I were muscular like him. My arms cross over my chest to cover it, but Jaden parts them.

"Please, let me admire your body for just a few more seconds," He begs. I blush, and he places his warm hands on each side of my waist, pulling me closer. My hands hang on my sides – I don't know what to do with them. I haven't been sober and naked in front of him before, and he's fully clothed. My heart is beating like crazy, and I can't control my breathing properly. He notices that and gives me a curious look before pulling away.

"Please, don't," is all I manage to say. I was barely audible.

"Sorry," he apologizes, and I realize that he has misunderstood my request.

"No, I mean... please don't stop touching me." I look up as the last two words slip out of my lips, and in less than a split-second, I'm getting pulled into a tight hug. He chuckles against my neck, and I feel my legs getting weak when his warm breath hits my skin. I ask him what he finds funny.

"Nothing. You are just too cute to handle," he whispers and kisses my earlobe softly before biting. I moan into his blonde hair.

We make out for what seems to be hours. Then, we both pull away to breathe, but only a few inches.

"Do you want to go for a swim after lunch?" Jaden asks and starts kissing down my neck and collarbone. I'm about to say yes when I remember that I have promised that time away already.

"I can't. I'm going for a walk with my mom," I tell him and sigh. I would much rather spend time with Jaden. I understand if he's disappointed, but he isn't at all. Why is he smiling?

"That's amazing!" he exclaims excited and kisses me quickly on the cheek. *What?*

"Boys, lunch is ready!" Judy shouts from downstairs, and Jaden opens the door. He asks if we should hang out afterward, and, of course, I want to.

He leaves our room, and I hurry to put on some comfy clothes – sweatpants and a gray t-shirt. I guess, I just have to survive the walk with Mom... before I can be alone with Jaden again.

CHAPTER FOURTEEN

"Here honey," my mom says, handing me a light blue hoodie she picked up from the grass. It's probably Jaden's. I thank her and put it on – it's definitely Jaden's. I can recognize his scent. We leave the others sitting around the long garden table.

Mom leads the way down the little path inside the forest that Jaden and I had walked on yesterday. There's silence between us, and I decide I have to ask her about something that has really annoyed me. "Why have you been so mad at me the last few days?" She turns her head to look at me; I look down at my feet as they move to avoid eye contact with her.

"Listen, Olly, I have been pretty moody because you've hurt me – a lot actually," she replies, leaving me confused. How did I hurt her?

"You came home out of nowhere, haven't spoken to me for three heartbreaking years, and now when you have finally come home, you haven't talked to me about how you feel or what you have been doing or anything. That's why I have been mad at you for the last few days," she stops. I can sense that she's about to cry. I'm so stupid. How could I have never thought about this? I stop walking, and this makes her stop too. I bring her in for a tight hug, at first she doesn't move. Then, she wraps her arms around me and starts weeping. I can't hold my own tears back now.

"I have missed you so much, Mom," I hear myself telling her. She dries her wet cheeks with her fingers.

"I have missed you too," she whispers and sits down against a big tree behind her. I sit down next to her. We're both silent for a few minutes, and then she starts talking softly.

"Tell me about how your life has been," She asks and nudges me with her elbow. How can I tell her without hurting her? She's has a mother's heart after all. I give up.

"So, I moved into a crappy apartment in town with Adam, who you have met, and four other *friends* – Britney, Jacob, Kevin, and Meghan." The last one still hurts when I say it out loud.

"Were they nice to you?" Mom asks softly, moving a strand of hair from my forehead. I think about her question for a few seconds. Were they nice to me?

"Mom, what you need to understand is that they don't do *nice*. Britney is an alcohol and drug addict, and when she didn't get what she wanted, she would become really mean. Jacob was always in a fight with somebody – not his *friends* though. He had beaten someone to death before, but there was no evidence, so he never went to jail for more than a week. Kevin sells illegal drugs and owes a ton of money to some bad guys. Meghan," I stop for a moment to breathe and wipe away the tears rolling down my cheeks.

"Meghan was amazing though. I always went to her when I was feeling homesick. She was my rock in the group. I told her – I tried to make her believe me – how absolutely amazing she was, but she wouldn't listen." I'm crying like crazy right now, and my mom pulls me closer.

"She harmed herself every night – every single night – right after she came home from having sex with some stranger... man or woman didn't matter as long as they paid. She was so beautiful, and she just let all those people touch her and hit her!" I scream through my tears and can't get air down my lungs properly. She whispers that I need to try and breathe in slowly. We do it together. I turn my head and notice that she is crying too.

"It will be alright, Olly," she tells me through her sobs and cups my face in her hands. Our eyes meet, and she gives me a smile.

I sit, my head leaning on her shoulder, for a few minutes in silence. She fidgets with her fingers – a habit I remember noticing when I was younger.

"What about Adam? Is he treating you... good?" she asks and makes my mind go blank. How did he treat me? If I compare it to the way Jaden treats me, then...

"The thing is... he doesn't like to commit to one person, so he kisses and has sex with a lot of guys, even though we are together," I try to explain and feel grossed out about myself. Why am I being with a guy who doesn't find enough in me?

"and how do you feel about that?" she continues, putting her hand on my shoulder.

"Not great, actually. I wish I could find someone who's in love with me – me only," I tell her, leaning back against the tree. Jaden loves me, but he's official with Arden, so that doesn't count.

"But you are still together?" she asks, and I sigh.

"We are, but I'm planning on breaking up with him very soon." As the words leave my lips, I feel a cold shiver run down my back. Jaden's words made me a bit nervous; not that I'll ever confess that. Mom nods and kisses my forehead.

"You deserve better," she tells me simply, getting up from the ground to dust her shorts. She pulls me up by my hands, and we laugh when I'm about to stumble over. I've missed her so badly.

We walk toward the others again, when she asks me the question I've feared. "Have you any plans for what you want to do after summer? I know it's late, but I'm sure we can figure something out."

"To be honest, I have no clue," I confess to her. She assures me that it's alright and that we will figure it out when we get home on Thursday.

The others are talking and laughing across the table – I love these people. Jaden looks up at me and notices my red eyes. He mimes if I'm okay, and I nod. I can't hold back a wide smile – I'm much better than okay.

"Olly, Kayla is coming in a bit, and then she and I will sleep here for the night, before leaving tomorrow morning. Is that okay with you?" Arden asks, smiling at me. I nod. What? I thought she would stay for the rest of the vacation... and I can't believe Kayla is coming as well. It's going to be a nice evening, and then... I can have Jaden all for myself tomorrow.

"Can I talk to you alone, Olly?" Jaden asks, pointing toward the forest with his thumb. The rest are dismantling the garden table. I nod, and we both get up. We walk away from the others in silence. I look back and see the girls looking at us, chuckling about something. What's so funny?

The tree crowns are almost neon green, and it feels magical. He suddenly stops after walking for quite a while and presses me gently against a tree.

I didn't see that coming. He stares intently at my lips. *Please* kiss me. He runs his fingers along my jawline. I'm impatient.

"I have missed you today," he whispers, leaning closer. I can't take it anymore and smash my lips against his for a sloppy kiss. I pull him closer, and our bodies move against each other. Our hands go everywhere, but it isn't enough... we both want more. His hands slip under my clothes.

"You look amazing in my hoodie. You can take it if you want to," he tells me, and I bring him in for another kiss.

"It won't be the same if it isn't yours." I bring my arms around his neck, and he smiles. We continue to share kisses and talk.

"Maybe we should go back to the others before they get all confused," I suggest, not really wanting to stop this moment. Actually, I remember what my mom said about how I haven't really been around since I moved back home, and I get that. Jaden nods and kisses me one last time before we walk back and start talking. I tell him about what happened on the walk with her, and he actually seems interested.

The day goes by fast. Arden, Sia, Jaden, Kayla (who arrived a bit ago), and I are standing in the kitchen and prepare the dinner. Jaden and Arden cut the vegetables, while Sia, Kayla, and I bake burger buns and forming the hamburgers so that our dads can put them on the grill. As we're talking and fooling around, I remember the reason why I loved spending time with Kayla back in the days, and she seems to remember too.

Jaden takes advantage of this and makes her tell funny stories of when I did or said something weird. He laughs loudly and jokes around. I don't mind. Even though I try to play hurt and offended, I really can't help myself from falling in love with him even more. I also love this, because it gives me the chance to make Sia tell me embarrassing stories from when Jaden was younger. I can't remember when I had last laughed this much.

CHAPTER FIFTEEN

Jaden is playing soccer with the boys outside, so I'm left alone with Kayla, Arden, Sia, and Katy upstairs in our room. We are pumping up two air mattresses – one for Kayla and one for me. I offered Arden my place in the double bed next to Jaden. I can survive one night without Jaden by my side. Also, it would be awkward if we – by habit – cuddle up to each other during the night, and Arden sees it. Katy isn't doing much; she is mostly lying on Sia's bed and looking at us crazy people trying to make the pump work. I guess we – the three girls and I – are hardly the perfect people for the job.

I throw myself on the double bed. I can't stop laughing... the expression on Kayla's face when the pump *finally* started working – priceless. Katy is giggling from the other end of the room. God, I feel so warm inside. Our moms walk inside with massive smiles on their faces.

"What are you guys doing up here?" Mom asks, laughing sweetly at us. None of us can answer; we are all crying with laughter now. Judy tells us that there will be dessert down by the lake in a few minutes, but we also have to put on some warm clothes. It's is getting colder outside.

It's a beautiful view of the lake, and I lean my head on Mom's shoulder. I'm sitting between her and Dad. I've been wanting to spend some more time with them both. It's so different now. I remember that small house we lived in when we were younger... Sam and I shared a room, and we didn't have a lot of money. Mom was so stressed out all the time. Man, it must have taken a lot to pull herself out of bed every morning for a job she didn't enjoy. Even Dad wasn't paid well for the job at the office. I'm so glad it isn't like that anymore – he looks so much happier now

"What are you thinking about son?" Dad asks and breaks my thoughts. I shrug and turn my head to smile at him.

"Not much, just about life in the old house," I tell him. He nods and tells me that he thinks about that time sometimes too. I ask him what he remembers the most.

"Probably our Saturday movie night, where we snuggled up on the couch – all four of us. I loved it so much. It was the one thing I looked forward to all week," he answers, taking a bite of cake on his plate that the girls had made. I can't believe that those nights meant so much to him; I wouldn't have made plans with Adam and the others almost every Saturday night if I knew. I feel bad now. He notices this and pulls me closer to hug sideways. My mom glances at us and smiles warmly before turning her attention back to Judy. Jaden is giving Arden a back massage on a blanket behind me – she has been feeling quite ill today.

CHAPTER SIXTEEN

I feel someone jump on top of my stomach. I open one of my eyes just slightly. Katy?

"Happy Birthday, Olly!" the little girl shouts, laughing excitedly. *My birthday?* She jumps down from the air mattress, and I sit up. All the others are in the room too – even Sam and his friend, who I haven't seen much of.

"Happy birthday, Olly!" they all shout together. I'm completely confused now. Is it my birthday? I ask them, and they all nod excitedly, and the girls giggle at my confusion.

"You turn 19, today!" my dad explains, and I nod to myself, realizing that I haven't celebrated any of my birthdays since I moved out.

"We guessed you had forgotten, so we decided to surprise you," Judy continues, and I glance over at Jaden staring at me. He smiles when our eyes meet but bites his lower lip to hold it back. He looks amazing – his hair is flat and undone, and his eyes look tired but full of joy. If we were alone... My thoughts are get interrupted by my dad. I look over at him. I'm not really hearing what he's saying, but I'm grateful he's interrupted my thoughts, because they were getting pretty steamy, and I know Jaden's were too.

"Your phone keeps ringing," Dad tells me. I look at the nightstand where my phone is getting charged. It's on silent, but the screen lights up. *Adam*. I stare at his nickname on the screen – Babe. I still haven't spoken to him or any of them since I left.

"Don't answer it, Olly," Jaden tells me, looking serious. Why can't he just trust me a bit? I unplug the phone and run my finger over the screen.

"Hey babe, before you hang up, please listen," Adam begs in a hurried voice. I haven't heard this voice in forever, but it sounds so familiar to me.

"Speak then," I tell him and look up at the people still standing in the room. I give them a soft smile. Jaden leaves the room. I hear him running down the stairs, forgetting that I have Adam on the line.

"I miss you so fucking badly... and the others do too. Why did you leave like that?" he asks, and I instantly feel bad. I could at least have told them where I was going and why? But, why did I leave?

"I just needed to get away from our lifestyle, I guess," I answer, not really sure what to say. I just didn't want to be around them anymore – but, I can't tell him that. He asks me when I'm coming back. I sigh deeply; I know he isn't going to like this answer.

"I'm not, Adam," I quickly answer, looking up at the others. They respect my privacy and leave the room. Charles tells me that I can come down when I'm ready and gives me one last soft smile before closing the door after him. There is silence on the other end of the phone for a bit, and it makes me worried.

"I should've seen it coming. Now that your parents have money, you think you're better than us. But, listen up – you are going to be lonely and miserable like you were before you met us. You are nothing without us, bitch!" he shouts, and I end the call with my trembling fingers. He's drunk. Fuck, I could almost smell the too well-known stench of alcohol drifting in through the phone. I'm scared; I'm trembling. As I throw away my phone, I'm crying. No. I can't be weak. He can't have that joy.

I'll get off the mattress. Ugh! The floor is cold... there are socks in the bag... and my black jeans and blue t-shirt. Why am I still crying? *Stop it*! I'll go to the bathroom... the mirror is dirty; my eyes are red and my cheeks are wet. *He* won. I'm crying. *Adam* won. My legs can't hold me up anymore. *Damn*. I sit down on the floor. I can't handle it – too many fucking emotions.

Shit, I'm lying down on the bathroom floor. I feel dizzy... tired... my legs are still shaking. I *need* to find Jaden.

Downstairs, everyone is sitting around the long table eating breakfast – except Jaden. Sia quickly notices who I'm looking for and tells me that he's down by the lake. I thank her and turn to leave when my mom asks me if I'm okay.

"No, not really. But, I'll be okay. I appreciate everything you guys do for me, but right now, I just need to talk to Jaden. I hope it's alright," I tell her, kiss her cheek and give her a tight hug. She smiles and nods.

I spot him sitting on the edge of the pier with his legs hanging down. I want to run over to him so badly as I get up on the lake pier... but, I hold myself back. He doesn't look back at me as I come closer; he's looking down at the clear water below him. I squat down behind him and wrap my arms around him. His shoulders tense for a second but then relax at my touch.

"Are you mad at me?" I whisper, giving him a quick kiss on his neck. He shakes his head and puts his arms around mine.

"You just deserve so much better!" he shouts silently into the fresh air. I sit down next to him; my legs are too tired to squat. I lean my head on his shoulder and sigh. I'm not sure if I do deserve better. I mean, I have put myself in this situation, so I have to pay I guess.

"I hope I didn't ruin your birthday; I just get so mad thinking about him. Sorry." He squeezes my thigh gently.

"You didn't, and neither did Adam," I tell him and put a hand on top of his hand lying on my thigh. He intertwines our fingers.

"Boys, come and say goodbye!" Kayla screams from the end of the pier. We both jump a bit, but then we get up and walks toward her. Oh! I remember... they are leaving now. Arden shows up on the path and runs toward us. She looks so happy, even though she still isn't feeling all that well.

"Have a safe drive," I tell them and hug them both tightly. Jaden and Arden kiss and hug for a bit, while Kayla and I are talking. We plan on having a sleepover very soon – just me and her – so that we can fully catch up.

We follow them to Kayla's car. They wish me happy birthday one last time, and we watch them drive away. I'm going to miss not having them for the rest of the trip, but I'm excited to be alone with Jaden. Just us.

Jaden turns to look at me and smiles widely. What is he up to?

"It's your special day today. So, I'm going to make you remember it!" he explains excitedly and leads me to his car. He opens the door for me like a gentleman, and I sit down on the passenger seat. Where are we going? Judy runs out to us and whispers something in Jaden's ear before standing back and waving us away. What is going on?

We drive by the yellow fields. We don't have any music playing because there's no signal, and neither of us have our phones on us. I realize now that I haven't really been on my phone this whole trip. I haven't even missed it, to be honest. I glance at Jaden who is talking about a cute little restaurant in town that has some alright breakfast.

"It can't be as good as yours though," I tell him and he smiles proudly.

"Of course not," he answers cockily, and we both laugh. He's so cute.

CHAPTER SEVENTEEN

"A table for two please," Jaden requests, and a young waitress leads us to a little table in the middle of the restaurant. There's a vase with beautiful flowers on the table. We sit down on each side, and she hands us a menu each. Jaden orders a glass of orange juice, and I order a glass of water. Jaden raises a brow at my order.

"No beer?" he asks me as the waitress leaves. I chuckle at his comment, and he smiles softly.

"I've realized that I don't need to drink all the time to make myself relax – I have you now," I tell him. He pulls out a white rose from the bouquet and presents it to me. I can't hold back a laugh. I have never been giving a flower before. He leans over the table and kisses me on the cheek. I blush like crazy and look around the restaurant – two waitresses are standing at a distance, giggling. They are both pretty young women in cute uniforms. The one that took our orders winks at me before placing our glasses on the table and writing down our orders. Jaden doesn't seem to have noticed anything. His eyes are on me.

"You two are the cutest couple I've ever seen," she remarks. I'm about to explain to her that we aren't together, but he replies before I can.

"Thanks," he answers simply and smiles at her. She walks away giggling. I look at him confused. He takes a sip of his juice and looks around like nothing happened.

"Why did you say that? Now she thinks we're together," I ask in confusion and take a sip of water. I wish we didn't have to lie about it though.

"I love the thought of you being mine," He retorts. He looks down at his glass shyly and plays with his fingers underneath the table. Is that one of the reasons why he hates Adam so much? Because he wants to have me for himself? I look around us – there's only an old lady with a little boy sitting at the other end of the restaurant. I decide to be a little spontaneous; he's always the one being so. I lean over the table so that our faces are only a few inches apart. I place two fingers under his chin and lift his head. He knows what I'm planning on doing and smiles sweetly. I press my lips against his and slowly kiss him over and over. He cups my face with his hands and pulls me a bit closer to deepen the kiss. We're getting interrupted by the waitress coughing quietly. I pull away and sit down on the chair again. She blushes and places two plates on the table.

"Hope you like it!" she mumbles and leaves our table shyly. Jaden chuckles. That was a bit awkward.

We sit in silence and eat, but I can't stop myself from glancing up at him every second. I notice him doing the same.

We pay and tip the waitress as an excuse for putting her in the awkward position and leave the restaurant. As we walk toward the car parked on the opposite side of the road, I ask him if he has anything planned for now. He nods excitedly and kisses me on the cheek before opening the car door for me. It has already been the best birthday in a long time. Then, Jaden jumps inside the car and starts driving. He checks the watch on his wrist.

"When did you start wearing an old man watch?" I ask jokingly, and he punches me on my shoulder. I pretend it hurts when it really didn't, and Jaden starts laughing.

"Since I had to plan my crush's birthday, but don't want to have my phone with me everywhere," he explains without taking his eyes off the deserted road in front of us. Did he just call me his *crush*? I turn my body slightly and lean toward his neck. I leave light kisses up and down, which form goosebumps on his warm skin.

"Stop it! I need to focus on driving," he complains, probably laughing to cover up the effect I have on him right now. I pull back a little, but I'm still very close to his skin. It's like if I'm scanning his beauty through a magnifying glass, every detail highlighted by the sun. I feel so lucky.

"Do you know what would make this birthday boy very happy?" I whisper in his ear, and he glances down at me, curiosity written all over his face.

"That we are completely alone tonight, just you and me under a duvet, cuddling up, kissing and..." I trail off, nibbling his earlobe.

"Other stuff," I finish. He bites his lower lip and tactfully assures me that he can make that happen.

We drive up beside the cottage. Jaden checks the watch again and smiles satisfied. What's up with him? We both walk out of the car, and he asks me to shut my eyes as we are standing at the front door. I do so. I can hear Jaden's knocks on the door, the door open, and then Judy mumbling something. What is happening?

"Come inside," Judy tells us, and Jaden leads me by my waist inside. He isn't even trying that hard to be secretive anymore. It's surprisingly colder in here, probably because of the air-conditioner. I still have my eyes closed as my dad shouts that I can open them.

Mom and Sia are proudly standing with a big cake in their hands. It's beautiful – Chocolate layers with whipped cream between them.

"We didn't really have the time to decorate it, but we hope it tastes good," Sia says, and I kiss them both on the cheek.

"I love it!" I say with cheer, and they both exhale in relief. I glance around the room – Sam and his friend are standing on the first step on the stairs, our dads are standing by the kitchen counter, and Jaden is standing beside me with Judy. Mom and Sia put the cake down on the dining table and quickly stick nineteen colorful candles in it. I love how they all put so much effort on this day – I mean, it's just my stupid birthday.

Sam gets the honor of lighting the candles, and everyone comes close to watch me when I blow them out. Sia reminds me to wish for something. I close my eyes and think for a second. I wish that one day Jaden and I can be officially together.

After eating and talking for a few hours, we decide to go down to the lake and play in the water. It's cold, but it doesn't matter. Everyone is in the water having fun. Jaden and I are playing around just to have an excuse to touch each other constantly. Our moms laugh at us.

"Arden ought to be worried. Soon, Olly will take her place," Judy shouts and makes everyone laugh. We both blush a bit but try to hide it. Are our feelings that obvious?

Jaden disappears for a moment to prepare the next surprise, and I help Sia prepare some snacks for the rest of them. They are going on a picnic. Jaden has planned with them that we aren't joining them, which even my mom seemed to be very okay with. I really think we are good again. Maybe, even better than before.

"Jaden likes you a lot," Sia suddenly states, and I blush brightly at her comment. I nod shyly and continue to put lids on containers with nuts and dried fruits.

"He's planning on coming out to our parents as soon as we get home on Thursday," she continues, which makes me frown. *Really?* I know that they will be all cool about it like they are with me, but it's still such a big, scary thing to do.

"How do you think Arden will react?" I ask, leaning on the counter. I must admit that I've been thinking about it for a pretty long time.

"She will be fine. Even though they have been together for this long, I know that she just wants what's best for Jaden," Sia explains and gives me a reassuring smile.

Someone comes running down the stairs. I turn around and see its Jaden.

"When are you guys leaving?" he asks Sia. Charles walks inside and tells him that they are leaving now. Jaden and I help her carry the snacks outside to one of the cars. We stand in the door and watch them drive away.

CHAPTER EIGHTEEN

I follow him upstairs and into our room.

"Stand here," he commands me and points to the front of the closed bathroom door. He kisses me gently on my lips and opens the door. It's dark in there; the light is switched off. I take a step inside and see the lit candles all around the room. The bathtub is filled with bubbles, and there are red rose petals in the water. My eyes slightly well up. It's so romantic. Jaden comes from behind me and puts his arm around my waist. I lean into his touch. He kisses my hair.

"Do you want me to get in with you or do you want to be alone with your thoughts for a bit?" he asks shyly.

"Of course, I want you to get in with me – I wouldn't want it any other way," I tell him, and he chuckles. He pulls off my t-shirt, and I turn around to do the same. I peck his lower lip, which makes him smile. We both take our pants and socks off and are only in our briefs. I pull him closer by the hips and kiss his forehead.

"Do you want to keep the briefs on or off?" I ask. I know he hasn't been completely naked in front of a guy before, and I want him to be as comfortable as possible. His muscles tighten; he seems nervous.

"On, for now," he simply answers, blushing slightly. I nod and bring our lips together; he deepens the kiss and relaxes a bit more.

We both get into the tub. It's not that big, so our legs lie on each side of the bathtub. I love the closeness between us. We lie in silence. His hand caresses one of my knees. I close my eyes and focus on the touch. I can hear his breathing calm down, and I smile. How can he make me so uncontrollably happy?

"Wake up, babe," I hear his calm voice whisper. His hands stroke my jaw. I open my eyes slowly, and his eyes meet mine. I put a wet hand behind his neck and pull him close until our lips touch. We share slow kisses.

"Thanks for making this day so amazing," I whisper, hugging him. We stay like this for a bit, and I notice that Jaden isn't in the tub anymore, he is squatting next to it. He's wearing blue jeans without a shirt on. I must say... it's a great view.

"You should probably get out of here before you turn into a raisin," Jaden comments, pulling away from our hug and chuckling. He helps me out and hands me a towel.

"I've laid out some fresh clothes for you on the sink, and lunch is almost ready downstairs. I'll be waiting for you in the kitchen," he tells me pecking my lips and walking out of the bathroom. *He's always prepared, isn't he?* I think to myself and laugh. I dry my body and put on the fresh briefs and jeans. There is no t-shirt – I guess that's a way of telling me that he doesn't want me to wear any.

I hurry downstairs; it smells lovely. He has made pasta for us, and we sit outside and eat it. We talk about weird memories from when we were younger – the first few involving pasta, but from thereon nothing to do with pasta or food in general. It's nice to look back at my childhood with positivity for once. I always used to think that everything was so terrible, but it really wasn't.

The others have come home now. I'm making puzzles with Katy and Sia on the dining table while Jaden prepares the last surprise of the day. He looks pretty nervous, and I can tell by the way Sia acts that she knows what the surprise is. Jaden comes down the stairs with two bags. What is he doing? I'm not the only one who's curious.

"Jaden, what are you doing with all of that?" Judy asks, and even Katy turns to see what he's carrying.

"It's a birthday surprise for Olly later," he answers simply before disappearing out of the front door. *Outside?* Sia smiles at me, which makes me blush slightly.

"He just bought a necklace for Arden – you're a special boy," Sia whispers over the table and winks. I blush even harder now.

Jaden leads me down the path to the treehouse. We hold hands and walk in silence.

"Climb up," he tells me and lets me climb up the ladder first. He seems nervous. It makes me want to hug him tight and kiss him so that he won't ever feel insecure around me again.

I go up the ladder but stop as my eyes peep inside. My heart starts beating a little faster – has he really prepared all of this? The mattress is covered with clean white sheets, there are candles burning in shot glasses, rose petals on the bed and… wait, is that a pack of condoms and a bottle of lube lying on the edge of the mattress. Whoa. Okay Olly, stop looking at that.

"Are you okay up there?" Jaden asks with a shaky voice from the foot of the ladder.

"Amazing," I breathe out, not really answering his question. I climb the last few steps and get inside. It's nice and warm in here. Jaden is getting inside too. He stands behind me, obviously nervous. I turn around and put my arms around his neck. I lean in and kiss him softly on his lips; he kisses back. I quickly pull off my shoes, and he does the same before we connect our lips again – this time it's more heated. I run my hands down his naked back and pull him closer. No shirts on, so there's only his jeans to remove. I zip down his jeans and lead him to the mattress. I push him gently on his back, put a hand on each side of his hips, and kiss him down the neck, torso, and stomach until I get to the jeans. He moans by the light touches, and my body responds immediately. I let my fingers follow the skin all the way to the button and pull the jeans off him. I throw them on the floor. He sits up, and I kiss him. He unzips my jeans and pulls them down to my knees. I take them off. He pulls me closer by my hips, keeping his hands there as he starts kissing and sucking on the skin, stopping right at the briefs.

I moan in pleasure and feel myself getting harder. He plants kisses – only thin fabric between his soft lips and my skin. My lips are slightly separated, and small gasps escape my mouth every time his lips touch my skin followed by his warm breath. I stop myself from pushing him backward and jumping on top of him, reminding myself that he hasn't done it with a boy before, and I have to be less rough. I'm not used to being gentle with Adam. Even though my first time wasn't anything special or gentle, I feel as if I have to protect him a bit and make sure his first time is. He pulls away a bit and stares up at me. I clasp his fingers and make him lie down on his back again. He bites his lower lip and closes his eyes.

"You're so perfect," I whisper and climb on top of him. He blushes, opening his eyes. Our lips meet. I leave kisses down his neck and suck a spot on his collarbone. He moans, tangling his fingers in my curls.

"Do you want to get under the duvet... you know, before we take off our briefs?" I ask softly, and he nods. I grab the condom and lube as we get under the white duvet. He leans back on his elbows, connecting our lips after we are half covered. I slip my tongue inside his mouth. His hands slide underneath my briefs while we share long kisses. I pull his briefs off completely, and my hand slides under the duvet. He pulls mine off too. His hands hold on tightly to the mattress, and he breathes heavily. My hand moves quicker.

I get on top of him and bite his ear. The condom is lying next to us. I grab it and peck him on the lips. I sit up, a knee on each side of his thighs. I open the condom with my teeth and throws the plastic on the floor.

"Will it be painful?" he asks, looking nervous. I roll the condom on and lean down, kissing him again.

"A little bit, but I'll do my best to make it as comfortable as possible," I tell him, and he kisses me passionately. I grab the bottle of lube and pull away a little. He removes the saliva on my lips with his thumbs and bites my lower lip. He moans. There's a sharp delicious pain in my stomach. "It feels so good," he breathes out, moving his hands from my hair and down my shoulders. He digs his nails into my skin.

"Are you ready?" I ask him in a raspy voice, and he nods. I lean in to his lips; he pulls me closer by the neck and slams our lips together, leading to open-mouthed sloppy kisses. I get inside him, careful to take it really slow, bit by bit. Jaden slowly eases in. We both moan into each other's mouths. It feels so good. Our chests rub against each other, and his fingers run through my hair again. We are breathing heavily, and I feel ecstatic.

"I love you so much," Jaden whispers against my lips, and I smile against his.

"I love you too," I tell him and gently bite his earlobe. I leave kisses down his neck. We both come, and I collapse beside him on the mattress. It makes me feel like the luckiest person on earth. He cuddles to my side, and we lay in silence, only hearing our own heavy breathing. I kiss him in his hair.

We clean ourselves with the sheets and put our clothes back on again. We're still not able to keep our hands off each other. I help Jaden pack the two bags again, and we head back to the cottage before the others start getting worried.

Later, we're all sitting on the couches in the lounge area watching a movie Sam had picked. I'm sitting between Jaden and Sam. There's a bunch of takeaway pizzas on the coffee table, but I'm not hungry. Jaden sighs quietly next to me and leans his head backward on the couch.

"How are you feeling?" I whisper, making sure that only Jaden can hear it. I remember how sore I was after my first time with Adam. But then, he was pretty rough, and I think I've done a better job with Jaden.

"Better than ever actually. I'm just so tired," he whispers back and yawns. It sounds adorable.

"That's normal. You can fall asleep on my shoulder if you want to," I reply. He leans his head on my shoulder shifting himself a bit before shutting his eyes. A few seconds later I can hear him snoring peacefully in my ear. I close my eyes too and rest my head against his.

CHAPTER NINETEEN

We were in the water almost all day yesterday and didn't really do anything else. It's the last full day before we leave the cottage tomorrow. I don't want to go home.

Sia, Jaden, and I sit upstairs in our room on the double bed. It's already late at night; the day went by too fast. We all ate lunch in town and went shopping, which gave me and Jaden a chance to sneak into a changing room and make out for a bit. Later, we had a lot of fun playing games in a park not far from here.

"Can you get the red wine from the kitchen?" Jaden asks Sia, and she sighs playfully before running downstairs. I grab the chance and turn to Jaden on the bed to press our lips together. It's not like we can't do this when she's around, we'll just feel awkward about it. I understand – Jaden isn't completely comfortable with his sexuality just yet, and she's his sister after all. Jaden moves closer, deepening the kiss. We get interrupted by Sia walking inside giggling and closing the door behind her with her foot.

"You're too cute!" she exclaims and places the wine bottle and glasses on the nightstand. Jaden pulls away and blushes heavily.

"Stop it!" he protests, and I can't hold back a laugh. He's *so* adorable when he's embarrassed. She jumps on the bed and shakes her nail polish. It's a nice shade of blue. Jaden opens the bottle and pours out a glass for each of us. The others are downstairs playing cards, so the three of us decided to spend some time together. Jaden hands me a glass.

"So, what are your plans after summer?" Sia asks me while opening the nail polish. I shrug and take a sip of my red wine. "I still don't know – I just don't want to go to school. It was a pain to finish high school," I tell her and sigh.

"What about something that involves playing the piano?" Jaden asks, and it makes me smile. It reminds me of Katy's birthday, and I can see on Jaden's face that he has the same pictures in his head.

"What are you two thinking about? You both smile like five-year olds," Sia laughs, and we join her. We don't answer her question, so she puts her focus on her nails again.

"But seriously, how about playing the piano at the theater your mom works at?" she suggests. I must say it sounds pretty cool. Jaden lies down on his stomach, and I fiddle with the t-shirt fabric between my fingers.

"I don't know if Mom would want me with her. I mean, it's like her own space, don't you think?" I ask them. Sia is already through with her nails and is blowing on them. A strong scent of nail polish spreads inside the room.

"No, absolutely not! I think she would love to spend more time with you," she answers and looks down at her nails satisfied. I lean over and look at them. They're beautiful – maybe a few mistakes here and there, but nothing big.

"Do you want me to paint your nails?" she asks, noticing my expression. I nod. I've never worn nail polish before. Jaden roll over on his back and looks surprised at me. I shrug and give him a quick kiss.

"What color?" she asks excitedly. I glance down at her nails again.

"The same as you," I answer, and she starts shaking it again.

All three of us lie on the bed half drunk and giggly. Jaden and I's fingers are entwined. Sia plays songs from her phone, fangirling over some singer whose name I didn't catch because of her high-pitched, fast words. I don't really listen; my focus is on Jaden's thumb caressing my hand. I love Sia, but I wish she would go downstairs, leaving Jaden and me alone for a bit. Jaden looks like he's thinking the same for he asks her if she didn't plan on skyping Kayla and Leah tonight. She frowns and then realizes what he meant. She grabs her computer and glass of wine and leaves the room, still smiling like a freak. She gives me a quick wink before closing the door.

The very next moment, Jaden gets on top of me and brings our lips together. Our lips move against each other in wet, passionate kisses. His fingers entangle in my hair. We both lie down on our side and cuddle close, not letting our lips part. I pull off his clothes, and he pulls off mine. We slide under the duvet, and I turn around so that Jaden can spoon me. I relax against his warm body while he softly kisses my neck.

I wake up hours later; the sun is shining through the curtains. I try to sit up but am pulled even closer by Jaden who still has his arms around me.

"I don't want to leave!" he protests in a husky morning voice.

"Me neither," I kiss his soft hand wrapped around me. I really don't want to go home – this place feels like paradise.

PART 3
-
AUTUMN

CHAPTER TWENTY

We drive through the town; it's almost deserted. I don't want to go home. I wish Dad would just turn around and drive back to the summer cottage. I feel tired, and it's only noon. I can't believe everyone is going back to their normal everyday life now, and I still don't know what to do with mine. The only thing I know is that I'm going to be around Jaden as much as possible – I miss him already, and we have only been apart a few hours. It's going to be tough. He's already starting soccer school on Monday, and then I'm going to be left here – lonely and miserable.

I can see our house in the distance. I can feel my heartbeat go up when I notice Jaden's car next to his parents' in front of their house. I can't wait to see him. As we come closer, we all notice that there's someone standing on the grass in front of our house. *Adam?* My body starts trembling, and my palms get all sweaty. Britney, Jacob, and Kevin are there too. The guys are arguing with Jaden, Sia, and Charles, while Britney's standing aside. I notice Judy take Katy inside the house from the car. They must have reached home just now.

My dad pulls up to the driveway and leaves the car with Sam. My mom turns around in the passenger seat to look at me.

"I think you should stay in the car," she tells me. I can see the fear in her eyes. I nod slowly in reply. I can tell that it makes her less worried. Her hand reaches out for mine and gives it a gently squeeze. I glance out of the window and get eye contact with Adam. He's staring at me with anger. I look over at their front door; Sam is getting let in by Judy, and Dad is walking over to Charles. I can only imagine how confused they must be. Kevin is shouting stupid stuff at Sia, but she doesn't seem to bother. I want to run over and tell them to get the fuck out of my life, but I know it would be stupid. Adam is more than just angry now, and it would surely be dangerous. I remember my talk with Jaden in the treehouse, and how I said that Adam wouldn't do me any harm – I'm not that sure anymore.

"Olly is my bitch!" is all I hear Adam shout before he's suddenly lying flat on the grass – Jaden gave him a solid fist directly on his face. Tears start streaming down my face. Mom squeezes my hand harder. I feel so embarrassed; Shit, I can't believe my mom just heard this. Jacob and Kevin storm toward Jaden, but our dads get in front of him. Dad gets kicked hard in the stomach by Kevin. I am steaming with anger; I want to get out of here so fast. Mom comes before me, jumps out of the car, and holds up her phone in the air.
"I'll call the police if you don't get the hell out of here right now!" she screams. I can hear the fear in her voice. Hearing this, the guys all get up and start running down the street.

Britney throws me a weak smile before turning around and following the others. I wish she could see that it doesn't have to be like this, that she can find happiness – like I have. Tears run down my cheeks uncontrollably. My head hurts, and I kick the passenger seat over and over as hard as I possibly can. I can hear Jaden say that he wants to talk to me, but my mom tells him to give me some time alone. I want him. I want him to hug me and kiss me and tell me that I'm his. I throw my head back and turn slightly – they are all stepping inside Judy and Charles' house. Are they mad at me? Why wouldn't they be? I have just got them into a fight that didn't even have anything to do with them. I *hate* myself. I should have just stayed with them; If I hadn't left, none of this would have happened... and they would still be living a peaceful life without any trouble.

"Olly, wake up, son. We're having the last barbecue for this year," I hear my dad whisper, and I open my eyes just a little. I fell asleep in the car. My eyes are still moist though, and I feel dizzy. My dad helps me out of the car. Why is he being so nice? Am I dreaming? He holds his stomach as I accidentally hit the sore spot with my arm.
"Sorry Dad, for everything," I tell him, still not completely sure if I'm awake or not. He softly kisses my forehead and tells me that it's alright and that I shouldn't feel sorry for anything. I *must* be dreaming.

He leads me to our neighbor's garden. Charles is standing by the barbecue. Sia, Katy, and our moms are cutting some vegetables at a long outdoor table – they all smile at me, and Mom gets up from her chair.

"Are you okay sweetie?" she asks, holding me in a tight embrace. I nod, not knowing what else to do. I'm not really okay, but if I say differently I might start crying, and I definitely don't want more of that right now. She sits down again, picks up the knife, and continues slicing cucumber. Dad is walking over to Charles who is standing by the barbecue. Jaden and Sam are playing soccer at the far end of the garden. I walk towards them; Jaden gives me a wide smile on noticing me and runs over to hug me. There's a scar on his lip, and his cheek is bruised. I want to cry so bad, but my head hurts by the thought of it – it can't handle this anymore.

"I'm so sorry," I tell him in a hushed voice. I feel so ashamed; it's all my fault. My eyes well up, but I dry them with my hands. Seeing this, Jaden tightens the hug.

"Please don't be," he begs, pulling away to look me in the eye. I'm trembling. It's dinner time, and I'm only wearing a t-shirt. I'm not ready for autumn.

"Here, take this," Jaden offers, pulling his hoodie over his head. The hoodie lifts his t-shirt with it, revealing his abs. I use this as a chance to touch him and pull the t-shirt down. He chuckles as my hands stroke his bare stomach. His blond hair becomes a mess after he takes off the hoodie. I laugh and am about to kiss him, but I remind myself that I can't. Jaden helps the hoodie over my head. I can do it myself – and we both know this – but it's an opportunity to be intimate. Sam, getting impatient behind us, sighs.

"Are you two lovebirds done so that I can beat Jaden in this round?" he asks, making both of us blush lightly. *Lovebirds?* I protest as a brother must, and Jaden continues playing. I walk back to the girls and sit around the table. I listen to Mom and Judy talk, but I'm not fully listening. I can't forget about Sam's comment. Lovebirds? Are we that obvious? And, if Sam noticed it, then the others certainly must have too. Mom, probably noticing that I'm absorbed in deep thoughts, gives my shoulders a light squeeze and smiles at me. I turn my head, and we catch each other's eye while she wipes away a curl from my forehead.

After dinner, Jaden and I left the others and came to my room. We're lying on my bed and talking. Jaden is breaking up with Arden tomorrow – they have a Friday-night date, and I can tell that he's nervous, even though he looks quite confident about his decision. I kiss him softly on the cheek, and he smiles. I love that smile – even with that scar on his lip. I move my eyes up his face and see his skin is bruised. I feel a mixture of sadness and anger – I need to break up with that asshole.

"Don't look at them. I can see the pain in your eyes, and I don't like it," Jaden says and kisses me. I deepen the kiss, knowing that we have to get down for dessert in a bit. He pushes me onto my back and gets on top of me. His nose strokes my ear, and he bites my earlobe. I gasp, and he softly laughs.

CHAPTER TWENTY-ONE

I check my phone for the fortieth time this morning. He hasn't answered my calls or texts in the last few days, and now I'm starting to worry. Did I say something wrong that Thursday, or is he secretly mad at me for not defending him in the fight against Adam? My phone lights up. I quickly grab it from my bed. Kayla. I had totally forgotten about our sleepover tonight. She has texted that she will be here in three hours. Shit. My thoughts have been completely on Jaden today; I'm not ready for a guest at all. On the other hand, what's there to prepare? I mean, we never really did anything big for them when we were younger.

I get up from my bed and walk downstairs. It's a Tuesday afternoon, and I'm home alone. Kayla, Arden, and Sia still have one more week off from school, so Kayla asked if she could come over. I'm extremely excited. How could I ever let my friendship with her end? She was the first one I came out to, and she was always so supportive, no matter what.

I open the fridge and the cupboards; there are no snacks at all. I consider going to town and buying some, but laziness kicks in. I walk upstairs again, get my phone, and call Mom.

"Hey, honey!" she speaks cheerfully. I can hear a lot of people talking in the background. They must be rehearsing for the Christmas Show at the theater.

"Hey, Mom, can you maybe buy some snacks on your way home for Kayla and I's sleepover tonight?" I ask.

"Yeah, sure! I'll be home at dinner time, and Dad will too, so we are going to order pizza" she explains. I can tell that she is busy dealing with others while she's talking to me.

"Cool... and thanks, you're the *best*!" I end the call, recalling that I always said this phrase when I was younger.

Kayla turns up in her little car and follows me upstairs to my room. She glances around my still un-unpacked room with boxes in the corners and smiles before letting her eyes fall on the filled shopping bags still standing next to my door after I went shopping with Jaden ages ago.

"Shouldn't you decorate the room with these things instead of hiding them in here?" she asks and pulls a candle out of one of the bags.

"I haven't had the time. Don't judge me!" I respond, raising my hands in defends. We both laugh.

"Oh, that's true... you have been busy with Jaden," she speaks, throwing herself back dramatically on my bed. Here we go! I jump in next to her and roll my eyes. She chuckles and winks at me before asking me how it's going between him and me. I explain that I haven't been able to get in touch with him for days, and she looks confused.

"Really? Maybe he's just busy with the new school and everything. He probably has a good reason" she assures me, and I nod in agreement. Why wouldn't he?

"But, he can't hide from me no longer because they are coming over for dinner on Thursday," I tell her. She rolls her eyes at my strategy – this is exactly like the old days, and I'm so happy. Although... I can't stop wondering why Jaden is ignoring me.

A few hours pass with the two of us just decorating and organizing my room with my old and new stuff. It feels really nice, and we just talk about really random stuff while doing it.

"I don't think we can fix this room anymore now... the pee colored walls will anyway kill the vibe," Kayla explains as we sit down with our back against the headboard and judge the room's poor potential. The word *fix* hits me hard, and I sigh, getting reminded of Jaden for the hundredth time today. Kayla turns her head to look at me.

"What are you sighing for? I'm sure it will look so much better if you just paint the walls all white," she speaks, and I can't hold back a laugh. I explain that it didn't have anything to do with the room. She looks at me confused, and I give her the whole 'fix-you' situation with Jaden in the kitchen. Her eyes widen, and she's about to say something, but the door opens, and my mom walks inside.

"Hey, Kayla! Nice to see you again," my mom says excitedly, and Kayla jumps off the bed and gives her a quick hug. I greet her as well and ask how her day at rehearsal went. She gives me a weak smile – I can guess the rest. She tells us that she has brought chocolate ice cream and a bag of chips for later. We thank her, and she leaves the room.

"What rehearsal?" Kayla asks as the door closes. I tell her that the theater arranges a Christmas show every year and that my mom has been given the responsibility for it to work out this year. She nods understanding, and we sit in silence for a few seconds before Kayla instead continues the conversation about Jaden... and me, of course.

"So, have you done it?" she asks curiously, and I blush, realizing what she just asked me. I throw a pillow at her head, and she laughs loudly.

"So, have you?" she asks again. I shyly nod, and she squeals in excitement. I feel my cheeks heat up and hide my face in another pillow.

"That's so sweet! Was it good?" she asks, trying to pull the pillow out of my hands. She's stronger than me and wins. I shyly nod again and picture that evening in my head. I miss him so much right now.

"Oh my God! When did you do it?" she asks loudly, jumping up and down on the bed in excitement. I ask her to be quiet – I don't want my parents and Sam to hear us.

"At the summer cottage on my birthday," I whisper, and her eyes widen. She's such a *girl* sometimes... and I love it.

"Give me all the details! Okay, maybe not *all* the details but like... you know what I mean" she pushes me, and we both laugh. I lie down on my back and start from the very morning and tell her everything until we fall asleep downstairs watching the movie. Kayla is hanging on to every word I say and stays quiet all along. Only a few dreamy sighs escape her mouth, and I must admit I enjoy telling her all about the day – I feel so lucky.

We get interrupted by my mom shouting from downstairs that we need to come down to the kitchen and decide what kind of pizza we want. We find a movie on Kayla's Netflix afterward, which of course *has* to be a cheesy romantic one, like the one we watch in the old days. I haven't watched one in forever.

The movie ends, and we glance down on the few slices left in the box; we don't normally eat that much.

"We are *officially* fat cows now!" she exclaims, and I stroke my stomach. It hasn't actually grown bigger.

We get the ice cream from downstairs and her stuff from the backseat of her. We lie down under our duvets on the bed, ice cream and spoons, and talk.

"Have you broken up with Adam yet?" she asks, digging into the container. I shake my head. Why haven't I done it yet? It's so stupid.

"Maybe that's why Jaden isn't talking to you. He wants you to break up with Adam before you two can go any further with your relationship," she reasons, and I can see her point. But, what about him and Arden? I guess one of us has to be the first to do it. I get up from the bed and grab my phone lying by the window. Kayla looks confused as I lie down again, looking for Adam under my contacts.

"I'm going to end it now," I declare. She smirks satisfied and moves closer to see what I'm texting.

"I'm breaking up with you, Adam. Have a great life," I read out loud and decide to delete the last sentence. This makes her smile widely. I press send and feel a little anxious, but I quickly push the phone away – he doesn't *own* me. Kayla wraps her arms around me, and we hug, both just staring at the phone screen. It's over.

CHAPTER TWENTY-TWO

I t smells lovely as I walk down the last few steps. I check my outfit in the long mirror hanging behind the front door in the hallway. Black skinny jeans – as always – and an olive green vintage shirt. Should I change into something else? I feel nervous. It's Thursday, and he has been ignoring me for a whole week – it's unbearable.

I enter the kitchen. My parents are running around, so I sneak away, not wanting to stand in their way. Sam is sitting on the couch watching television. I sit down next to him. He's looking nice, and so are my parents. It's apparently a pretty formal dinner. The company that my dad and Charles are working for is expanding to Europe. So, they are going on an exciting business trip very soon. Well, I don't really get why we're celebrating, because they are going to be away for quite a while.

My thoughts are interrupted by the sound of our doorbell. Sam hurries up and gets the door open. It's followed by small talk and laughs. I turn off the television and take a deep breath before walking to the opening into the hallway. My heart is beating, and my palms are sweating as I see Jaden standing at the front door. He's wearing a pair of nice blue jeans and a white long-sleeved t-shirt with a little black logo on the chest; his blond hair is flat, and he looks tired. My mom gives him a hug; our eyes meet over her shoulder. He gives me a weak smile.

What's going on? Sia storms toward me and kisses my cheek; her dark lipstick probably left a mark. I've missed the sweet smell of her perfume. Katy is a bit shy and is hanging by her dad's leg all the way to the living room. Judy and Charles both hug me, and I feel warmed by their love.

Jaden and I are left alone in the hallway. He chuckles as he sees my cheek and walks closer. He licks his thumb and gently tries to remove the lipstick; his other hand is resting on my shoulder.

"You've been quiet lately," I start, deciding to open my mouth. His eyes look down at the tiles, and his hands fall down his sides. I miss his touch already.

"Boys, food is ready!" My mom shouts from inside. Typical. Jaden looks up at me with an empty expression on his face and walks past me into the living room. *What?* I don't get him.

Throughout dinner, I talk mostly to Sia sitting in front of me. Jaden is completely quiet; sometimes, he glances at me from across the table, but then he continues to ignore my presence. I feel like crying. I can't believe it; after *all* the things we've been through.

I get up from my chair and walk upstairs. If I sit there for two more seconds, I'll go completely insane. I walk into my bathroom and close the door. The ice-cold water hits my face. He probably has a good reason for acting like this, I keep telling myself, but I'm starting to doubt this. Is he just tired of me? I hear footsteps coming up the stairs and quickly dry my face with a towel.

"Are you up here?" a soft voice asks me from the little corridor between the bathroom and my room. Jaden. I open the door and see him standing in my room. He turns around and notices me.

"Hey, are you okay?" he asks. I walk inside and close the door after me. He sits down on the edge of my bed. I take a deep breath, feeling all the emotions bubbling up inside me. "No, Jaden, I'm not! You have been ignoring me for a week! Do you think this is a game? I broke up with Adam. It's over. I want you, but you don't seem to feel the same way about me!" I yell, and my eyes start to water. His do too. He stands up and pulls me into a hug. His embrace shows that he cares for me, but I can *feel* that something is up. I pull myself away from his arms. I need answers right now, not his hugs.

"I couldn't do it," he whispers, and his eyes start to water heavily.

"I couldn't break up with her – I can't hurt her like that," he cries. Is that what all of this is about? He doesn't have to break up with her just now. I pull him closer and kiss him. His cheeks are wet under my hands. He pulls away.

"I can't be with you before my relationship with Arden is over. Sorry," he explains, looking down. My heart sinks. The first few words keep repeating in my head.

"When is that?" I ask, in a slightly shaky voice and keep my eyes on his... ready for whatever answer he's going to give. A hope inside of me begs that he will say a few days or even weeks – I just need to know that it isn't over forever.

"I don't know, Olly," he whispers softly, tears streaming down his cheeks. His face becomes blurry. Gaah, all these fucking tears. He takes a small step toward me and wipes his thumbs over the soft skin below my eyes. I lean my forehead against his chest; my whole body is shaking.

"Please... don't do this" I manage to say through my sobs. I put my arms around his waist and take in his scent. I know that I'm going to miss it very soon. He puts his arms around me too and kisses my hair.

"I have to. I can't live with myself if I don't let you go now... this has already been going on for too long," he tells me between his sobs and tightens his grip around me one last time before pulling away. I thought he was in love with me.

"But what about your plan? I thought you were going to... fix me!" I shout after him as he starts his way out of my room. It's my last desperate attempt to make him stay; but, he just smiles weakly.

"You don't need me anymore... you are so strong and so amazing... and you deserve better than an asshole... or a confused straight guy in your life," he finishes before disappearing down the stairs. I do need him still; I need him more than ever now before I start shouting in my head – but the words don't leave my mouth. He has made a decision, and there's nothing I can do about it. I sit down on the edge of my bed. My mind can't put the puzzle together, and my body has no clue how to react either. Tears keep streaming down, and I can feel a massive headache taking over my brain. What is left without him? What have I done wrong? God did he *ever* even love me? I push the last question away though – I know he did... does.

Not much later, I'm again sitting on the chair around the dining table. Mom called me down for dessert, and my eyes are only slightly red, but enough for all the women to notice and throw me confused looks. Both dads, Sam, and Jaden are outside, playing soccer in the garden and mom has only just asked them to come inside again.

Sam, Charles, and Dad are all walking inside the living room. Where's Jaden? Judy must have thought the same thing and asked them about it. Charles explains that he wasn't feeling well and went home. This makes both moms exchange sad looks.

CHAPTER TWENTY-THREE

We drive up to Sam's school – just Dad and me. We are going to have a boys-only day at the mall, and even though I'm still down from last night, I feel like I owe Sam some quality time with his elder brother – that's the least I can do.

"There he comes!" Dad exclaims, and I look out of the window to witness what seems like a thousand kids running out of the big doors of the school. It throws back memories from when I went to school here. I would hurry out of the school like that too, ready for the weekend to start. Sam, after saying bye to his group of friends, enters the car. I'm happy he isn't a loner like I was.

We enter the mall after walking what felt like a mile because Dad, of course, had to park the car at the other end of town. My heart starts beating a little faster – not much, just a little – not because of anxiety, but for the memories with Jaden – how he helped me like the gentleman he truly is.

"I'm going to look for something nice to wear for the business trip, but you two can just hang out somewhere in here, okay? I'll call you two when I'm done, and then we can agree on a place to meet?" he speaks, and we both nod. He disappears down a street, and we stand in silence for a moment. I realize that I haven't had any time alone with him for years. It feels so weird.

"We can find a place to sit in the little café down there," he suggests and points down a street. I agree and follow him down the street, trying to ignore the many people walking around me. *They are not judging you – stop fucking around with me, brain*!

"Are you coming?" Sam asks softly, standing behind the glass door on the way inside to the little café. I didn't even realize that I had stopped walking. He sends me a little smile and gestures with his hand to make me follow him. I feel a bit embarrassed that my little brother, who's only ten years old, has to babysit me in some weird way.

It smells strongly of coffee, and my mouth starts to water. The café is small, and all the walls are black chalkboards with cute and simple drawings and quotes. This is cozy, and it reminds me of Brooks Café – stop constantly thinking about him! I slap myself mentally and sit down in a booth in front of Sam.

"What are you thinking about all the time?" he asks curiously, and I look down at the table and fail to try and stop myself from blushing. *Jaden*, I scream inside.

"A guy, to be completely honest with you," I tell him, and his eyes widen. If I want us to get closer, I need to open up to him. He starts smiling, and we both laugh at the awkward moment. Some of the people sitting around us glance at us.

Sam asks me if we should get something to eat. I look up at the menu written on one of the chalkboard walls. I'm actually pretty hungry; I haven't eaten anything today. He seems to have made a decision – so I ask him what he's planning on getting.

"The brownie and hot chocolate look really good, so I think I'm going to get that. What about you?" He pulls out his wallet from his black raincoat and stands up. He looks so mature, and I feel kind of guilty not really knowing why.

"Um, just the same as you then," I say with an unsure voice and pull out a credit card from my denim jacket. My dad gave it to me last night so that I have some money until I get a job. Those were his exact words – *until you get a job*. We both know that that probably isn't going to happen in the near or far future.

I stand up too, and Sam looks confused at me.

"I'll buy, just stay here," I tell him. He's about to protest, but he stops himself and sits down in the booth again. As I walk up to the counter, I can't help but feel proud of myself. For a lot of people this might seem stupid, but being able to buy something for my little brother like this is a rare moment. I want to make this more of a habit.

As I come back to Sam, he's sitting with his phone in his hand, texting someone. I glance over his shoulder and notice the red hearts after the texts.

"Whoa! Who deserves all of those hearts?" I ask him, placing the tray with our brownies and mugs on the table. He quickly switches off his phone and looks down at the wooden table.

"Just a girl from my class," he answers quietly and coughs awkwardly. I take a sip and can't hold back a smile when his cheeks turn a dark shade of red. I want to ask a thousand question, but I remember back to when I was younger, and my parents would do it... it was the scariest and most embarrassing thing in the world. I think I'd better control myself.

"What's her name?" I softly ask, not wanting to push him too much. He tells me that her name is Maya, and she just started in his class after summer break this week. We start eating our brownies and stop talking, but that it isn't very silent though, because the café is getting pretty crowded now, and the sound of people talking are merging together to become one loud noise.

"She is just so confusing sometimes," he suddenly speaks and follows with a sigh. I look up at him. He stares into his mug with an unhappy expression. Oh, I know this feeling only too well.

"The guy I like is too," I tell him, and my mind takes me back to last night. *Stop it!* Sam looks up from his hot chocolate, and we look into each other's eyes. It looks like he just found the last piece of his puzzle.

"Is it Ja..." he gets interrupted by his phone ringing in his pocket. Was he just going to say Jaden or is it just my brain playing games with me? Has he noticed the flirtation between us?

"It's Dad," He tells me, bringing the phone to his ear. My thoughts are rushing around, and I feel overwhelmed. What will I answer if he asks me? The sound of spoons clinking in mugs are getting louder now, and a woman's laugh echoes between my ears. Sam snaps me out of my thoughts.

"Did you listen? Dad wants us to come and help him pick a nice suit," he says, emptying his mug. I still haven't eaten much of my brownie, but I have suddenly lost my appetite. So, I just leave it be.

We enter a huge fancy store at the very end of a street among other expensive-looking stores. Chandeliers are hanging down from the ceiling, and ironed suits are arranged on long racks. I look around and see Dad facing a rack at the other end, talking to a young shop assistant. Sam sees them too, and we walk over to them.

"Hey boys!" Dad greets, noticing us. The shop assistant turns around to look at us. He's probably in his early twenties; he's wearing a nice pair of black pants, and a nice white shirt. He is extremely handsome. He smiles at me, and I feel very unconfident.

"These are my sons – Sam and Olly," he introduces us to the handsome guy. He stretches out his hand for me, and I shake it. What is that weird, intense feeling between us? He *must* be gay. Dad and the guy whose name tag says Phillip shows us the three suits they have in mind.

"Have you tried them on yet?" Sam asks, and Dad shakes his head; he tells us that he wanted to wait till we came. He walks into the dressing room and leaves us standing alone with Phillip. I glance down at Sam, and I can tell that he feels awkward too. He starts walking around the store, feeling the sleeves as he runs his hand over the expensive material hanging on the racks.

I look over at Phillip, only to notice that he's already staring at me. I feel the heat rushing to my cheeks but ignore it to my fullest ability – I'm not going to stand here blushing like a thirteen years old little girl.

"Nice outfit," he remarks with a soft smile, after sizing me up for way too long. I glance down at my clothes and lightly chuckle. I'm wearing a pair of ripped, black skinny jeans, a white t-shirt with a vintage-ish denim jacket on top that is way too big for me. Nice outfit? Really? He didn't even sound rude. I want to give him a compliment in return, just to be polite, but I can't think of anything. To my luck, Dad pulls the curtain to the side and draws our attention toward him instead.

Phillip wants him to try on the blue one again; so, Dad reenters the dressing room. I check the time on my phone; we have been looking at suits for an hour now, and I'm getting really impatient. Can't he just choose one? They all look the fucking same anyway. I groan out loud and lean against the wall next to the dressing room.

"How old are you, Olly?" Phillip suddenly asks, and I look up and meet his eyes staring into mine.

"19, you?" I speak, feeling a little nervous talking to him. He just seems so... formal?

"23. Do you have a boyfriend?" He answers and almost makes me choke. Did he just ask me that? Am I that obviously gay?

"I don't... what about you?" My heart aches as I think about Jaden again. It's just impossible to get him out of my mind. Phillip tells me that he doesn't have a boyfriend either, and I'm afraid that the next question is going to be something like a date or my phone number, but luckily, Dad pulls the curtains to the side. Sam walks in closer to me; he has been walking around the store for a while, and I can sense that he's getting impatient too.

My eyes widen as Dad pays Phillip for the suit. One thousand dollars for one damn suit that he's going to wear just once! My jacket was ten dollars in the local thrift shop, and I have worn it at least one hundred times in the four years that I have owned it. It doesn't make any sense. Phillip writes something with a pen on the receipt before handing it to Dad.

"Have a nice day and good luck with the business trip," he tells Dad and winks at me. If he knew that I'm not thinking about him right now, he would be pretty disappointed. Yes, he's hot... but nothing compared to Jaden. Maybe I need to realize that I can't have Jaden anymore.

We walk down the parking lot looking for the car. Why did he have to park so far away from the mall? Dad looks down at the receipt and chuckles.

"Olly, call me," he reads out loud in a high-pitched voice that makes Sam laugh. He hands me the paper. A number is written below the note. I feel flattered; I just wish he hadn't given it to my dad.

"Are you calling him later?" Dad asks as we enter the car. I glance down at the phone number.

"No, I kind of like someone else," I explain. Dad starts the car, and I can hear Sam mumbling something from behind me. I can't hear what though, and I'm not sure if I want to.

There's silence in the car for the first few minutes, and I worry what Dad is thinking about.

"It's not that guy Adam, is it? Because, I don't feel good about you being with him," he speaks softly, avoiding eye contact.

"No Dad, it isn't him, and thanks for being protective sometimes. It fits you," I answer so quietly that Sam couldn't possibly have heard it.

"I just want my boys to be happy," He squeezes my knee and smiles at Sam through the rear-view mirror.

CHAPTER TWENTY-FOUR

I walk downstairs. It's Saturday, 10 am. My head feels heavy and my body empty. I cried myself to sleep last night, and a spinning headache is creeping up on me.

Mom, Dad, and Sam are sitting around the dining table.

"Look who decided to join us!" Mom shouts cheerfully and pats the chair next to her. I sit down and notice that Dad looks visibly tired. I ask him why.

"I drove Jaden home from the hospital this morning because Charles and Judy are visiting his grandparents this weekend," he answers, and my heart starts pounding in shock.

"Was Jaden at the hospital?!" I shout. I could feel my eyes almost pop out of my skull, not believing the words I heard.

"Olly, relax. Jaden wasn't hospitalized. Breathe," Mom tells me, placing her hand on my tense shoulder. I exhale all the air I was holding on to.

"It's Arden who is. She got hospitalized the day after we came home from the summer cottage, and Jaden has been visiting her every day since," Dad explains, and my heart sinks.

"Why?" I ask, hoping that it isn't anything bad. Mom puts a slice of bread on the plate in front of me, but I don't feel like eating anything.

"She has a very serious illness," Dad explains, and Sam looks up in surprise with wide eyes. Serious? Dad places his arm around him and kisses his hair. I understand now why Jaden has been off lately. He must be devastated; she means so much to him.

"I know you are concerned about him. I think you should go talk to him after breakfast," Mom suggests and runs her hand through my morning hair.

"He doesn't need me and doesn't want to talk to me," I spit back. I didn't mean for it to come out so cold.

"No? Is that why he asked me how you were doing before he fell asleep in the car?" Dad says and makes me blush. Maybe, he hasn't *completely* forgotten about me, I think in relief. However, I can't get the terrible thought of Arden in a hospital bed out of my head. I get up from my chair. Jaden needs someone to talk to... rather he wants me to do it.

"Honey, eat some breakfast first," Mom tells me, pouring out some apple juice in a glass for me. I sit down, not really in the mood to eat. I want to see him now. Even though the fear of getting rejected is playing on my mind, I try my best to ignore it.

Mom and Dad clear the table, and Sam runs upstairs to change; he has soccer training today. I put my plate in the sink and leave a quick kiss on my mom's cheek before walking out of the hallway. I put on my sneakers and a gray hoodie.

It's cold outside, and the air is humid after last night's rain. Even, the grass is wet. I knock on the door with my cold knuckles, and it almost echoes.

"Olly, I haven't seen you in ages!" Sia shouts, pulling me in for a tight hug as always. I step inside the hallway and take my sneakers off. Neither of us speak for a minute. I hope he's home.

"He's in his room sleeping, but you can just wake him up," she tells me and ruffles my hair with a smile before disappearing into their living room. I walk upstairs. My heart is beating faster, and my feet feel heavy on the steps. What if he tells me to leave?

I enter his room, and the door creaks. I hold my breath and glance inside. My eyes water a little when I see him lying under his duvet. He's snoring peacefully. I walk inside and close the door behind me. My heartbeat gets faster as I sit down on the bed, inches from his warm body. His lips are slightly separated. My hand, still cold, reaches out and touches his warm cheek. His eyelids flicker a few times. His eyes open and reveal his beautiful blue eyes. They widen at first, but then they soften again.

"Olly?" he asks in a sleepy voice, but before I can answer, his lips touch mine. Not kissing, just our warm breaths meeting each other. He pulls me up on top of him. I squeeze my lips around his lower lip, and he moans softly. His hands cup my face, and mine rests on each side of his stomach. Hot kisses follow. He pulls me down next to him on the bed and gets up on top of me. His eyes light up. And all this while, I thought that he didn't want to see me. I hold his blond hair and tangle my fingers in it. His lips slide down my neck and gently bite my skin. Moans escape my lips. I can't even think clear anymore. He pulls away, falling on his back next to me. We lie in silence. I can only hear our heavy breathing.

"Why didn't you tell me about Arden? I could've been there for you," I ask, finally getting to what I came here for. He sighs and turns to face me; I turn too.

"Because our relationship doesn't work that way. You aren't meant to be taking care of me. I'm always the one protecting you, and I like it that way," he answers calmly, and our eyes meet. He caresses my cheek with his warm hand.

"You will always be my hero. I won't see you weak and helpless all of a sudden," I whisper, feeling a tear roll down my cheek and touch his hand. He leans in closer and kisses my forehead.

"I love you," he declares. He pulls me under his warm duvet. I cuddle up to his side, and he puts an arm around me.

"I love you too," I whisper back, relaxing into his touch.

CHAPTER TWENTY-FIVE

It's Sunday, and Dad is leaving after dinner. He and I are the only ones home, because mom is at the theater, and Sam is in school. We used all morning moving the piano from the living room upstairs to my room and grocery shopping for tonight. I have been visiting Jaden every day for the last two weeks after he's back from school and checked up on Arden at the hospital. But today, I'm not. I have decided to spend the whole day with Dad.

"Can you cut the unions?" Dad asks as we enter the kitchen. I nod, and he looks for a knife and cutting board for me. I remember when I was younger, I would sit on the kitchen counter in the old house and tell him about my day, while he would cook dinner. It was a magical time from my childhood. I ask him what we are cooking, and he smiles proudly before opening the fridge. He pulls out a package with four huge raw steaks and bottle of red wine. Dad has always been a nerd when it came to food and wine, but it fits him better now, where he seems to have the resources for this lifestyle.

"I think we need to taste this baby before pouring it into the sauce," he laughs and gets two wine glasses from a cupboard. I'm going to miss him so badly.

My eyes are burning and watering uncontrollably. I hate cutting onions. I take a step back from the cutting board and put the knife down. I wipe the tears with my sleeves.

"Are you crying because you are going to miss your old man?" Dad jokes and makes a funny face at me. I laugh, poking him on his stomach. He pokes back.

"Stop it!" I cry, feeling ticklish, but I can't stop laughing. The front door opens, and Mom enters the kitchen. I run over and hide behind her, still laughing.

"What are you two doing?" she asks, chuckling at us.

"We're cooking dinner," Dad answers acting innocent, and all three of us laugh. Mom tells us that she left the theater a little early today so that we can get the best out of the time Dad's home. I kiss her on the cheek and continue cutting the unions. She walks over to Dad who is fixing up the meat and kisses him.

"This looks delicious!" Mom exclaims, glancing over his shoulder.

Sam and I both help Mom clear the table after dinner while Dad gets his suitcases from their bedroom. I put the plates in the dishwasher. The time is getting too close now. Mom glances over at me from the sink, and I can see that she is thinking the same.

He comes down the stairs. Sam helps him carry the baggage down the last few steps.

"Careful, we don't want anyone to fall," Mom says, and I follow her out to the hallway. I open the front door for them. Judy, Sia, Katy, and Charles are standing by their car and Dad greets them. We walk over to them, and Dad puts his baggage in the trunk of their car. They are driving together. I glance around. Where's Jaden? I ask Judy.

"Arden is doing worse, so he's a bit of a mess today, but I'm sure he would want to talk to you. He's in our garden," she tells me, and Sia gives me a weak smile from behind her.

"But before you run off, you're going to say goodbye to your dad," Mom says. I was actually about to forget this – that boy takes away all of my focus. I give Dad a long hug, and he reminds me to call him if I need to talk. I give Charles a hug too and wish them a great trip. I won't see them again before Christmas.

I find Jaden standing at the end of their garden kicking a soccer ball repeatedly into a goal. I move closer to him. He looks tired and angry.

"Hey," I say softly, and he notices me. He kicks the ball into the corner of the goal and leaves it there this time.

"Hey," He answers, walks hesitantly toward me. His eyes are red, and his cheeks look wet. He has been crying. I pull him into a hug, and he quickly wraps his arms around me. He breaks down in tears and starts to breathe heavily. His weight feels heavy for me, but I ignore it. He needs a hero too.

"I can't do this. I can't do this against Arden," he suddenly says through his tears in short breaths. I pull away to look at his eyes. What is he saying? We get eye contact, but it feels like his eyes are empty.

"What do you mean?" I ask, getting scared by my own weak and shaking voice. I don't sound like a hero at all.

"Every time I look at her, I feel so guilty. I'm cheating on her. I'm cheating on the most amazing girl I know, and I can't do it anymore. Arden needs me," he tells me, drying his eyes with his bare cold hands. I feel numb. What is he saying? He can't be ending it again! I hear the sound of a car starting and driving off. No! This isn't happening. It can't be. Jaden turns around and gets the ball from the goal. He puts it down on the grass again. I follow every move he makes.

"I want you to leave Olly," he says with a shaky voice, keeping his eyes on the ball before kicking it into the goal forcefully.

CHAPTER TWENTY-SIX

My mind feels empty and muddled. Tears flow endlessly. The bed feels hard against my weak body. I want Dad to come home again, and I want Jaden to tell me that we can still be together. I want his warm lips and his embrace and make all the pain go away. I mentally hit myself in my face; Arden is at the hospital fighting for her life, and I want her boyfriend to lie next to me, cuddle me, and tell me that everything is going to be alright. I hate myself now. A tear runs down my cheek and on my lips. Salty shame.

"Baby, don't cry," Mom whispers and strokes my hair with her motherly hand. She is sitting at the edge of my bed in her nightgown. She probably heard me cry on her way to bed. I just hope Sam can't hear it; there's no reason for him to worry.

"Do you want to sleep in my bed for the night. I don't like the thought of you lying up here alone and crying," Mom asks, pushing the duvet off me. I don't protest; I can really use my mom's comfort tonight. We tiptoe down the little staircase from my room. The floor on the first floor is warmer.

I feel safe under Dad's light duvet. Mom holds my hand, and I close my eyes, but only for a few seconds. The bedroom door opens. Sam is standing there with his own duvet; he's crying quietly.

"Hey sweetie, come here and lie down between us – there's space enough," she whispers and pats the spot between us. We let go of each other's hands and move a little to make more space for him. He lies down, and Mom wraps an arm around his waist. I hold his hand, and he tightens his grip on mine before closing his eyes. I close mine too.

"Goodnight boys," Mom says softly, and I drift into a deep sleep.

CHAPTER TWENTY-SEVEN

I lie and listen to Sam's snoring. The bedroom door opens,

and Mom walks inside. I sit up and notice that she's carrying a big wooden tray.

"I thought we deserve breakfast in bed today," she explains, placing the tray at the end of the bed. I poke Sam gently, and his eyes open slightly.

"Mom's made us breakfast," I whisper, and he slowly sits up too. We lean against the headboard and dig into the delicious food mom has cooked for us, as she reads out loud a long text from dad for us. He tells us that they are on the plane and are going to land very soon and that he misses us a lot already. Sam tears up a little, and I put an arm around him. I hate seeing him sad.

"Okay boys, the clock is ten minutes past seven. Sam, I will drive you to school, and Olly, you can come with me to the theater if you want to. We are leaving in thirty minutes!" Mom shouts from downstairs. Sam jumps up from the bed and goes into his room. Did she just ask me if I want to come with her to work? I mean, why not? She did mention that they have a nice piano there.

I jump up from the bed and run upstairs to my room. I feel rested; a feeling that I've missed. I find something nice to wear – I don't want to embarrass my mom – and jump into the shower. I think about last night and this morning, and a thought strikes me. How did I ever decide to leave all of this for an idiot who treated me like shit and an apartment where I didn't feel safe or comfortable except when I was high or really drunk? Even with the pain coming along with my relationship with Jaden, I don't regret coming back home, because all the love he has given me will forever overshadow the pain and uncertainty. He's having a hard time right now, but I haven't given up on him. I'll give him the space he needs, and hopefully, he will come to me when he's ready.

We leave the house. Sam jumps to the backseat of the car, so I'll have the passenger seat.

"Ready?" she asks and starts the car. We both nod, and she starts driving. I take my phone out of my jacket pocket and unlock it. I haven't checked my phone in two days. A few texts show up – one from dad asking how I'm doing; I text him back instantly, informing him that I'm good, but I miss him a lot in many words. There's one from Kayla, asking me what I'm up to and when we should hang out again; I will call her later. And then, two texts from Adam – one saying that he wants me to consider coming back to him. Hasn't he gotten wiser? The next text gets me choked.

So you like the fancy guys now. I should tell you that Phillip wants you to call him.

I stop breathing, and my heart beats faster. How does he know that?

"Are you okay, honey?" Mom asks me after saying goodbye to Sam at the school parking lot. I nod, not being able to get words out. I know Adam way too well. He's done this trick with other guys before, and it never ends well for the other person. I get shivers but try to hide the fear. I don't want mom to worry about me.

We decide to buy lunch on our way to the theater. She parks the car in front of a little shop, and I ask her if I can call Kayla.

"Sure, what do you want me to buy for you?" she asks, opening the car door. I ask her to get two of what she wants, and she leaves. I find Kayla in my contacts and call her. I need to get distracted. It rings many times before she picks up.

"Hey!" she speaks, and I can feel her smiling like crazy.

"Hey, where are you?" I ask her and click my seatbelt off so that I can sit in a more comfortable position. She giggles, and it echoes.

"In the school bathroom with Leah. We were in class when you called, so we sneaked out. What are you up to?" she says. I remember Leah. The last time I saw her was at Sia and Jaden's party back in spring.

"I'm heading to the theater my mom works at with her, and right now she is buying us some lunch for later," I tell them. Kayla asks me if I've heard about Arden, and they give me more details of her illness and how she's doing.

"Arden told me the other day that she wants you to come and visit her at the hospital someday. She misses you," Leah tells me, which makes me feel really guilty.

"I will," I answer. Kayla changes the subject to my relief. I need them to cheer me up, which they do by telling me about school and weird classmates.

Mom comes out of the shop with a plastic bag in her hand. I had hoped the girls would make me forget about Adam's text, but I still can't stop thinking about it.

We enter the big old building. It's beautiful. Mom tells me that she has a meeting scheduled.

"But, you can just take a look around, and then I'll find you when I'm done, okay?" she says, and I nod, not listening fully since my phone lights up. It's a picture from Adam, A half-naked selfie in bed. He doesn't even look that good. I quickly turn off my phone and put it back in my pocket. I'm going to have a nice day with my lovely mom, and he isn't going to ruin that.

I'm amazed by the dark corridors and cables hanging down from the ceiling. It's exactly what I imagined it to be. I walk down the corridor and up an old-ish staircase. It's very narrow and creaks as I step on it.

The loft room is brightly lit. There are many racks with costumes in different colors, a table with a sewing-machine on top of it, and an old chair. A window in the pitched room has a narrow opening, and the wind blowing in makes the costumes dance. I feel the fabric on a dress with my hand; it's obvious that the costumes are for the Christmas show.

"You're Olly, right?" a low voice comes from behind me. I turn around and see an old lady standing on the last step on the staircase. I nod and take a step away from the costumes; I don't want her to think that I was prying, even though I kind of was.

"Did you sew the costumes?" I ask politely. She smiles warmly at me and walks over to them. She is wearing a long olive-green dress with laces at the hem and on the sleeves. Her gray hair is tied up in a bun, and only a few wisps hang down her face. Her lips are dark red.

"I have. Do you like them?" she asks and takes out the dress I was touching of the rack.

"Yeah, they're beautiful," I tell her, and she smiles at me again. I glance around the room; it's so cozy up here. She grabs my hand; it's warm and wrinkly. I follow her down the stairs. Where are we heading? She doesn't walk fast, and her heels create a pleasant sound as they hit the floor. We walk down the dark corridor I was in just before. She lets go of my hand as she enters through a big open door. Cables are taped to the wooden floor, and I realize that we are standing on the grand stage. I look at the empty seats; they form a nice and uniform pattern.

There's a vintage-ish piano standing on the right side of the stage, a few meters away from the props, a few bare trees and a snowman.

"How rude, I haven't even introduced myself yet. My name is Eleanor," she laughs and gives my hand a light squeeze before letting go. She walks over to the piano and sits down on the bench in front of it.

"It's a very beautiful building," I compliment. By the way she looks around as if it's her home, something tells me that she has a very strong connection to this place.

"Thank you," She says quietly, and it echoes in the big hall.

I walk over to the piano and run my hands over the nice wood. It's amazing. She adjusts the papers with notes. Her nails are long and painted dark purple. She places her fingers on a few keys and presses down. She closes her eyes, exactly like I do.

"Do you play?" I ask her, and she nods, with her eyes closed still. Her fingers dance over the keys and make it looks effortless; she must be pretty practiced. I close my eyes too and take in the sound. My body leans against the piano. She stops playing, and I open my eyes. Eleanor smiles at me and pats the spot next to herself on the bench.

"Do you want to try?" she asks, moving to the edge of the bench, giving space for me to sit down.

She reads out the notes for me, and I put my fingers on the keys. I mess up a few times, but she doesn't laugh at me. I feel calm around her. She reminds me of my grandmother. My mom's parents died in a car accident when I was around seven, and my dad's parents didn't ever want to have anything to do with Sam and me. So, I'm not used to being around older people a lot. She smells of flowers and shampoo.

My mom and the kids who are performing in the show enters the stage and interrupt us in our playing. I leave the stage and find a seat. They are practicing. Eleanor is playing perfectly; the kids are making a few mistakes, but there's still a long time till Christmas.

CHAPTER TWENTY-EIGHT

It's Friday, and I have been with mom at the theater all week. It's great here. Everyone is nice to me, maybe because I'm her son and people seem to like her. Eleanor teaches me to play when she gets time. I have gotten really good at playing the notes for the show, and I have taken a copy of them so that I can practice over the weekend.

Mom is talking to Judy on the phone as we enter the car. She looks at me more serious than before; her eyes are staring me down. I feel weird. She doesn't look particularly angry – more scared or sad maybe. She ends the call.

"What's going on mom?" I ask her, and she smiles her motherly smile at me and strokes my cheek. But, her smile fades away too quickly.

"Judy told me that Sia has just called her, saying that Jaden got really mad about a text from Adam and smashed his hand on one of his bedroom walls and then ran off to fight Adam," she tells me. My heart sinks. This is *bad*. What could he have texted that made him that angry?

"Judy doesn't know where he is now, but he texted her saying that she shouldn't worry," she continues, keeping her eyes on me. I stare out of the window. It's all my fault. She asks me if I have any idea where he could be. I shake my head. I just hope he isn't in pain. Mom starts the car and leaves the parking lot. I'm silent, but in my mind, I'm screaming.

I run upstairs; I need to call Jaden. I enter my room and whoa! He's sitting on my bed. I almost jump in shock, but I'm just relieved that he's here in my room safe and under my supervision. He is wearing my headphones and staring down on his phone. He doesn't seem to notice my presence. I want to jump into his arms and kiss him, but I'm not sure why he's here. I move closer to the bed. I'm not mentally ready, but I can't control myself. My shadow comes over him, and he looks up at me. His face looks horribly bruised, and his upper lip is broken. Anger is running through my veins. I feel so frustrated and guilty – why am I going through the exact same feeling again?

"Did Adam do this to you?" I ask him after he takes off my headphones. He stands up.

"They all did this to me, but I didn't react gently... so don't get mad," he answers, making me sit down on the bed. I ask him what Adam texted him. At first, he looks confused, probably because I know that there was a text message involved. I tell him that Judy called my mom, and it was Mom who told me.

"He messaged me saying that he would force you back to him, and if you resisted, he would harm you," he blurts out harshly, and his eyes are dark. My body feels heavy on the bedding, and I feel dizzy. Jaden was right from the beginning – Adam wants to harm me. My hands tremble in fear. I know how cold-hearted he can get, and Jaden's face is the proof. I look down at Jaden's hands. One of them is, as Judy told my mom, scraped from smashing it into his bedroom wall. I take his hand in mine and strokes his wrist carefully, making sure that I don't touch his sore skin.

"I couldn't let him hurt you," he whispers and brings his other hand to my cheek. I don't deserve someone like Jaden. My whole body is trembling, and a tear escapes my eye.

"I don't want you to get hurt either... but look at yourself," I cry, and he gently dries my eyes with his thumb.

"I know... I'm fine though," he tells me and lifts my chin so that our eyes meet.

"How can you be fine?" I ask, wanting him to show me some other emotion. He can't be this calm; it doesn't make any sense.

"Because I know you are safe now. I could see it in his eyes – he gave up. You will be safe from now on," he tells me and kisses my forehead. I'm safe. I jump up from my bed and hold his warm body in an embrace.

"Thanks, you're my hero," I cry into his neck, and he strokes my back. How does he steal my heart so successfully every time I'm near him?

"I just want you to be happy. Even when I can't be with you, you're still mine," he whispers, pulling away only to connect our lips the same second. Even after a while, our lips still fit perfectly together, moving in a slow but intense tempo.

"As soon as Arden is healthy, I'll break up with her," Jaden whispers against my lips, "and then I'll come out to my family and be yours forever," he continues. *If* Arden gets healthy.

We hear talking downstairs. It's Judy and Sia who are talking to mom. We run downstairs. Sia is holding Katy, and Judy is crying and hugging my mom.

"Mom, don't cry," Jaden says, and Judy turns around. They hug, and Sia gives me a weak smile. I smile to Katy, who looks very confused. She smiles back at me and giggles.

"Don't ever do a stunt like that again, okay?" Judy tells Jaden in a firm but caring voice, and he nods.

"I'll make dinner, and then we can play a movie and cuddle up on the couches... deal?" Mom asks and makes Sia chuckle as Katy gets all excited.

CHAPTER TWENTY-NINE

It's Thursday, and I'm with Mom at work like every other day these last two weeks. Eleanor is sitting in the front row; I'm playing her the whole Christmas show. I've been practicing non-stop. I glance down at the notes lying in front of me a few times, but I've got them pretty much memorized.

I press my finger on the final key, and Eleanor stands up applauding. I smile shyly at her and chuckle. I know I made a few mistakes, but nothing big.

"Come and sit down next to me," she shouts and pats the seat next to hers. I jump down from the stage and sit down.

"I have played in the Christmas show for the last eight years now, and I'm starting to get a little bored... and I just don't feel like performing this year. So... if you want to take my spot at the piano, you can," she says. I feel elated and get sweaty palms. I look up at the massive stage and down the almost endless seats.

"They won't look as scary when you first start playing," she assures me, placing a hand on my knee. I nod and try to ignore the fear building up inside of me. I did it at Katy's birthday; I can do it again.

"I would love to," I finally tell her, and she squeezes my knee before letting go. She pulls me into a hug, and I can't stop smiling.

"Did you ask him?" mom asks from behind Eleanor. I look up over her shoulder. Mom is standing at the door frame. Eleanor pulls away from the hug and turns around. She nods at mom. Mom looks over at me to find out what I answered; I smile, and this lets her know.

"Amazing, honey. Now, you basically work here!" she smiles and walks over to me. I get up from the seat and hug her. Do I have a job? I remember not believing I would find something to do after summer. Look at me now, having a job that I actually enjoy going to. I *have* to call Jaden.

Mom and Eleanor begin talking about some pertinent things. I leave the room and walk upstairs into the loft room. My phone is lying on the desk where I left it after talking to Eleanor this morning. I can't stop smiling as I find him in my contacts. He's going to be so happy.

"Jaden, you'll never guess what just happened," I tell him, a little into the conversation. His voice is husky as he chuckles at my excitement. It echoes. He told me earlier that he's standing in a bathroom at the hospital. Arden is soon coming out of surgery, so he's going to be there when she wakes up. He should have been to school, but he has an agreement with the school leader at the moment that he can visit her as long as he makes sure to keep up with his homework.

"What happened, then?" Jaden asks. I bite my lip, trying to stop smiling, but I give up. I tell him, imagining his clear blue eyes full of joy.

"That's so cool! I can't wait to see you play at the show. You are going to absolutely *kill* it," he whispers excited, and I hear some people walking past the bathroom.

"I hope so," I tell him and sit down on the chair in front of the desk and lean back. There's silence for a few seconds. Jaden yawns, and it sounds so adorable.

"How long did you sleep last night?" I ask him softly, already knowing that it wasn't a lot. He sighs and groans.

"Not much, maybe three hours," he answers. I wish I could cuddle up next to him every night and make him sleep peacefully, but I can't because he will feel guilty and even worse than he is right now. The silence repeats itself.

"I dreamt about you though," he whispers, and my cheeks flush by the thought of it. I ask him about it.

"That we drove off to the summer cottage and stayed there, just you and me, cooking dinner and snuggling up on the couch that quickly evolved..." he trails off, and I bite my lip. I often dream about him, but I actually didn't expect him to dream about me, seeing that he's so busy and stressed. I feel flattered... and a little turned on.

"I miss you," I whisper and bite my finger. He chuckles and tells me that he misses me too. He has to go now, and we end the call. I can't wait to see him.

"Who were you talking to?" Mom asks. She stands on the last step on the staircase and smiles at me. I wonder how much she heard and kind of want to disappear from the situation.

"Um, just some guy," I answer and shyly run a hand through my curls. I really hope she will let the conversation end here.

"Okay... is he... handsome?" she asks and fiddles with her fingers. This is so awkward. I nod and blush. *Please* don't ask more questions.

"Shall we head home?" she asks. Okay, I can live with this question. I get up from the chair and follow her out. What a nice day.

CHAPTER THIRTY

I can hear light footsteps coming up the narrow stairs. I know this sound way too well. The door opens carefully, and his dark shadow appears in my room in the moonlight shining through the curtains.

"Why aren't you sleeping, babe?" he whispers and takes off his sneakers at the door. He's wearing his black soccer training shorts and a navy-blue hoodie.

"I can't fall asleep, but more importantly, why aren't you sleeping? You have the trials for the professional team tomorrow." I ask, and he drops himself next to me on the bed. He runs a hand through my curly hair and moves closer.

"I couldn't fall asleep. It's painful how much I've missed you," he whispers and kisses me passionately on the mouth. I kiss back slowly but carelessly – we're both pretty drained.

"Do you want to go for a walk? I know it's three, but I can't fall asleep right now," he asks, staring into my eyes. It's dark, but I can just see the silhouette of his face as he speaks. I escape his eyes and turn around to glance out of the window. It doesn't look that cold.

"We can go for a small walk, but then you have got to get some sleep. Deal?" He nods and gives me a quick peck on my lips before getting up from the bed. I'm lying under my warm duvet in briefs only and don't want to get up. I groan and ask him to find some clothes for me in the little closet. He grinds his teeth at my groaning. His sleep schedule is a complete mess.

It's extremely cold outside, but what did I expect? It's a November night. This boy can convince me to do anything with those gorgeous blue eyes. We walk down the little path we've walked through before into the forest that morning with Buffy and coffee.

"How did the surgery go?" I ask softly, not wanting to push him too hard to talk about it if he isn't ready yet. He puts his hands inside his hoodie pockets.

"Very well. The doctors told me that she will be okay soon," he answers in a low, shaky voice. I glance over at him. His eyes are wet, but he's holding back the tears. Why does he always have to be so strong? Just let loose for once! I link my arms with him and lightly lean against his arm.

"That's good," I whisper back and kiss the navy-blue fabric. He stops walking and turns to look at me. There aren't any lights; the moon shines weakly, but I can see his jawline and puffy lips clearly.

"Why have we stopped walking?" I ask. He pulls his hands out of his pocket and weaves our fingers together. He leans in closer and makes our foreheads touch. His eyes are dark, and his fingers squeeze mine a little harder.

"I just wanted to look at you and admire your beauty," he speaks in a husky voice against my lips. My legs turn weak underneath, and I kiss him. Everything from now on happens in slow motion. Our hands let go of each other just to find each other's cold bodies quickly. I notice our breaths in the cold air. I run my fingers through his blond hair on his nape. His hands grab my hips with lust, and I moan against his mouth.

"I don't think this will help me fall asleep, now that I'm just turned on," Jaden laughs and kisses me down my neck. I gasp and tug his hair trying to control myself.

"Should we stop then?" I ask begging that he will continue just a little longer, even though it's pretty selfish of me. He chuckles against my neck, and my stomach hurts as his breath hits my skin.

"Are you crazy?" he moves away from my neck and looks into my eyes. "This makes me more relaxed than some stupid sleep," he continues and connects our lips again. I bring my hands to his chest and try to get him closer by tugging on his t-shirt. He smiles against my lips. He's the best thing that has ever happened to me.

CHAPTER THIRTY-ONE

Kayla chuckles at a meme on her phone. I look away from the road and peek over her shoulder.

"You have such a basic humor," I laugh, and she sticks her tongue out at me. We are both tired; we didn't sleep a lot last night. It was probably a stupid idea to binge-watch Christmas movies till early morning, but it's kind of okay because we're near the very end of November now. It's stupid though because we're going to visit Arden at the hospital today. Kayla yawns and takes a sip of my coffee. She makes a face; she doesn't drink coffee.

"It's disgusting. How can you drink this weird liquid?" she complains and coughs. I laugh at her, and she hits me playfully on my shoulder.

A nurse leads the way for us through the long plain hallways. I hate the smell of hospitals, so I inhale the scent of the flowers we bought at the gift shop. Kayla smiles at me; she probably remembers me complaining about it when we were younger because one of our teachers always smelled of hospital.

"That's her room. She's been excited for your company all week," the nurse tells us, pointing at a light blue door on our left. We thank her, and she walks away. Kayla opens the door, and we walk inside.

"Hey, friends!" she shouts from her bed at the end of the little room. She stretches out her hand as a sign for us to give her a hug.

"Hey, love! How are you doing?" I ask and hug her; Kayla does too. I show her the flowers, and she brings them up under her nose.

"I'm doing better and thank you so much for these. You absolutely didn't have to," she says and hugs us again. I've missed her a lot. Kayla leaves the room with the flowers to find a vase for them, and I'm left alone with Arden. I sit down on a little chair next to the bed, and she starts telling me about her treatment. I feel my whole body tense up when she talks about the medicines and the surgeries. I'm not sure if I would have been able to handle it myself. She doesn't look sad though; her skin is pale, and her eyes look tired, but she seems... *happy*?

"Enough about me, what are you up to at the moment?" she asks, leaning her head on her palms.

"Um, I play piano at the theater my mom works at,"

"Jaden told me that you're going to play at the Christmas show this year. That's exciting!" she says cheerfully and motions her hands like she's partying. Has he told her?

"Okay, party girl, you need to calm down a bit," Kayla laughs as she enters the door. She places the vase with flowers on the nightstand and sits down on the other side of the bed.

"Have you heard... our boy is a musician now?" Arden asks, clapping her hands. I blush at her excitement; I didn't expect a crazy reaction like this.

"Yeah, he told me on our way here. I'm so proud of him!" she answers and claps too. I hide my red face in my hands. Arden stops clapping and turns a little more serious as she looks at me.

"Jaden has been going through a rough time lately," she starts, and I look up at her, "and I know that he's finding some peace when he's around you. So, thank you for being there for him. I know it means a lot to him," She tells me, grabbing my hand. I give her a weak smile. Guilt. Too much guilt. I can't take it. I'm trying to hold back all the bad feelings. She doesn't know anything. Jaden and I's first kiss at the party, our time at the cottage... And she's been sick all along, knowing nothing.

"Of course," I whisper, not being able to do anything else. The shame is slowly killing me, and sweat is creeping up on me. Kayla gives me a weird look, but Arden doesn't seem to notice, luckily. They start talking about how school is because Arden obviously hasn't been there for a while. I don't listen fully; I'm trying to remember what Sia told me in the summer cottage... something about how she just wants Jaden to be happy. I swallow stiffly and hold my breath for the rest of the visit.

Water is flowing down my naked chest. Shame. Guilt. I turn up the heat, begging to be washed clean. How has Jaden lived with this feeling for so long? My whole body is drowning in soap, but I still feel dirty. His innocent soul, his body I couldn't stop touching every chance I got, and his golden heart. I can't breathe properly because of the thick dampness in the little bathroom. I lean against the tiled wall; tears flow through my already red eyes, and I slide down the wall until I'm sitting on the floor. Water pours down harshly on my sensitive skin. If I just hadn't fallen in love with him. What if she finds out about us? She would never ever forgive me.

He's so terribly perfect! I hate him so badly! Why couldn't he have just left me alone? I was better without him. Instead of fixing me, he has ruined me... he ruined me even more than how damaged I was before I'd met him. I'm a mess because of him and his crazy love. I clench my teeth. How can I still want him though? I try to imagine Arden sitting in her hospital bed; it doesn't help me much. I need his arms around me. His comforting words and his kisses.

"Olly, you've been in there for an hour now. Are you okay?" Mom shouts from outside my bathroom. I quickly wipe my tears back and clear out my throat.

"Yeah, I'm fine," I shout back, trying to stop my voice from cracking. I want her to hug me, to kick the door open and recognize that I'm not okay; that I'm bleeding from the inside, look me in my eyes, and notice the pain.

"Okay, I'll go to bed. Sleep tight," she tells me, leaves down the stairs, and closes the door after her at the end. I'm alone. I'm stronger alone. I turn off the water, but my tears won't stop. I don't need him. I'm tired of having these feelings – of missing dad, of being taken care of. I don't need them; I want to go back to my past. I miss Adam and the others. They didn't constantly check up on me. They didn't notice when my head was hanging low a bit. I want to be Adam's boyfriend again, but of course, Jaden had to ruin that as well. He ruined me.

CHAPTER THIRTY-TWO

Silence. The pizza is warming in the oven. 19 years.

Congrats Sia... oh, and Jaden. Mom looked disappointed when I told her I wasn't going to celebrate their birthday. It's just a stupid birthday dinner. My phone starts ringing for the thousandth time today – I know it's him. I'm not going to answer or put it on silence; I enjoy hearing it ring – the thought of his disappointed face on the other end. I don't care. I'm officially *not* feeling anything anymore. If I don't want to get hurt, I won't get hurt. Easy.

Knocks on the door. It opens. I glance down at our little hallway. Sia. Relieved. I, for a second, feared Jaden would be standing there.

"What's going on?" she asks and gives me a disappointed look. I have seen too many of these. She leans against the kitchen counter and stares at me. I don't answer her.

"Kayla told me that you acted strange on your way home from the hospital a few days ago," she continues. I still don't answer, just shrug my shoulders. Please leave me alone.

"I can get Jaden to come over here if you want to talk to him instead," she offers, but I shake my head. I don't need to talk to anyone. I glance down at the oven. The pizza is done, and so is this conversation.

"Will you please talk to me?" she begs and walks closer to me. I take a few steps back. Our eyes meet; she looks worried. If I had never shown up here, they wouldn't have to spend all this energy on me. We would all have gone on with our lives without each other. I would probably lay on the sofa in the apartment, playing video games with the guys, drinking and smoking, not worrying about anything. These days, I worry about everything. I want to go back and stop the pain for all of us – the pain that has existed ever since I showed up.

"I want you to leave, and I want you to tell Jaden that he should stop calling me, because I'm not going to answer," I say coldly, feeling a tear rolling down my cheek. It hurts a lot more when I say it out loud. Sia slowly steps back with tears in her eyes too.

"I can tell him to stop, but he won't, because he loves you, and so do I," she whispers and turns around. My heart is beating, and I'm blinded by the tears building up in my eyes. I hear the door close. I can smell something burn. Great. I use my sleeves to dry my eyes, and I open the oven. Warm air hits me in the face. The pizza is as hard as a stone and uneatable. My stomach churns.

I look through the cupboards. There it is... Bottles of wine and vodka. I'll grab the one with the highest percentage of alcohol in it. Alcohol – the only thing that can numb my feelings right now. I open it as quickly as possible and starts drinking from the bottle. No more emotions. I'm done with feeling anything anymore.

The alcohol warms my blood. I grab my phone from the counter. Fifteen missed calls from Jaden just today. I want to hurt him. Not answering his calls won't put him in pain.

A crazy idea comes to me. I press the number. I shake slightly, but I ignore it; it's just the alcohol. Ah! The recognizable voice, the good ol' days. I'm nervous, but ask him where they are hanging. It's not far away.

It isn't cold outside. Christmas lights are hanging in every garden down the streets. It's the first day of December tomorrow. I have a plan – I'm going to make sure I'm back home in the apartment before Christmas day... when they'll all stay in the summer cottage again. I'm not a part of the family. Tears roll down my cheeks, and I stumble over something and land on the ground. The bottle of vodka shatters as it hits the ground. Fuck. Shards of glass fly everywhere. I try to stand up, but trip and put my hands on the broken glass. It cuts my cold hands in a few places. Blood is dripping. It sticks in my hands, but I get up and continue walking.

They are at the skate park. There's Adam, sitting on a bench by himself. The others are lying on the concrete, probably high. Britney sees me and gets up on her feet.
"Olly!" she screams excited and is about to run over to me, but Adam holds his arm up at her, and she stops. He's staring at me. Is that anger? It can't be. I walk closer to him. Why would he tell me where they are if he didn't want me to come? He stares me up and down.

"Come and sit down," he orders in a raw voice, patting the spot next to him on the bench. I smile. He looks amazing. As I sit down, I look over at Britney. Her eyes are distant and cold, but her lips curve into a weak smile. I've missed that smile. The other boys don't notice me, but that's fine. Adam's left hand slides over my thighs and in between them. His other hand turns my head to make our eyes meet. He leans in closer and bites my earlobe roughly. Ugh! It hurts and starts whirring at my ear.

"Have you missed me, bitch?" he whispers furiously. My mind feels numb, and blood starts dripping from my ear and down on the bench... small drips... a few seconds in between each drop. He smashes our lips together, forces his tongue inside. My eyes water... Ugh! I feel like throwing up every time his tongue hits the back of my throat. His hands grip my jeans, unzips them. His breath smells sour. His skin and hair are oily. He smells of sweat. His hands are dirty. I pull away.

"Please... stop," I whisper desperately, but he drags me back. His dirty hands find their way between my jeans and my briefs.

"I thought you wanted to play?" he bites back. I'm bawling my eyes out. Britney starts laughing. I look over at her; she is staring at the sky. Why doesn't she help me? I feel like screaming for help, but no one would react. Adam moans against my lips with closed eyes. My whole body is shaking. I want to go home to Mom. His grip is so strong, I can barely move. I can't believe this asshole is laughing at me. Fuck I was happy to see him. So stupid of me. I get up; his hands fall to his sides. He spits after me; I start running.

My legs are weak, and I have no energy or even the desire to stop these tears. What have I done? I feel sober, but my body is drunk as fuck. He shouts nasty things after me, and the others laugh with him. I can't hear what he's shouting; all sounds are getting mixed together. Am I going crazy? I try to zip up my jeans, but I constantly lose balance and give up.

The lights are on at home. Fuck. I trip over a rock in our driveway. Someone comes running behind me. Jaden.

"What's happened?" he asks worriedly. He tries to pull me up. His eyes turn wide when he notices my opened pants and bleeding hands and ear.

"Please, don't touch me," I cry. I don't want him to see me like this. He loosens his grip on me, and I try to walk myself... but I can't. I've fallen again. He tries to help me up, but I push him away. His eyes are full of fear and confusion.

"Where is he?" he asks, looking at my unzipped jeans. I want to hit him, but I don't have control over my body. The front door opens, and Mom comes running outside.

"What's going on?" she asks softly, but she is about to faint as she comes closer and sees the situation. Embarrassment. I throw up on the ground, and Jaden tries to help me again.

"Don't *touch* me! I don't want anyone to touch me! And don't try to find him Jaden... I went to him myself!" I scream, trying to stand up. This time, a little more successfully. Mom grips my arms, ignoring my complaints. Jaden doesn't move; only tears roll down his cheek.

"Why would you do that?" he asks in a shaky low voice. I look away, and Mom helps me up the steps to the front door.

"I don't belong here," I whisper, and mom pulls me into her arms.

"Of course, you belong here," Mom says and shakes her head as she runs her fingers through my hair. I don't believe her. This is all wrong. Mom is wrong. Me coming here was wrong. *Jaden* was wrong. Jaden. My eyes meet Jaden's.

"And, I can't be fixed," I say, feebly. He looks down at the ground and nods. No no, don't give up on me. I need you to see that I need you to force me to let to you stay. He turns around and walks home. I watch him walk. *FIX ME, PLEASE!*

PART 4
-
WINTER

CHAPTER THRITY-THREE

It's Sunday morning, December 7th, and it's snowing outside. I take hesitant steps down the stairs from my room. I haven't really spoken to anyone other than Mom since last Sunday. The scene keeps replaying in my head, and I feel sick again. My body is screaming at me, but more so my mind. Can't I just hide in my room forever?

Mom has decorated every corner of the house for Christmas. She peeked her head into my room the other day and asked if I wanted to join her. But, along with every other thing, she asked me about working, and I said no.

Mom and Sam are sitting at the table. The tempting smell of bacon and baked bread hits me, and my mouth starts to water. I glance over at the kitchen.

"Dad!" I shout and run over to him. He pulls me into a hug. I didn't know he'd come home already.

"Why didn't you tell me that you were home?" I ask him, and we pull away. He smiles at me and hands me a kitchen bowl for the table.

"Because when I walked into your room a few hours ago, you were sleeping heavily, and Mom told me that you hadn't gotten a lot of sleep over the last week. So, I didn't wake you up," he explains, and we both join the others at the table.

I did actually sleep last night, which felt nice. I think it was because I finally sat down with Mom and told her everything. It was scary, really scary. She knows everything now about Jaden and me and what happened on Sunday night, but she's promised not to tell anyone about any of it. If Jaden is coming out of the closet, he has to be the first one to tell people. I'm still pretty mad at him, but the anger gets weaker every second I think about him.

I glance up at Mom and find out that she's already looking at me. She smiles warmly at me, and I smile back. I feel empty inside a lot, but I don't want to. I want to be happy and love people. I want all kinds of feelings, even the scary ones.

"Arden came home from the hospital yesterday," Mom suddenly tells me, and I freeze. What? I look around at the others who are smiling at the good news. I lean back on the chair. I can't believe it.

"She still has to go for weekly observations, but she can start in school again and everything," Mom continues and puts some food on her plate. I can't stop smiling. That's amazing. Dad looks over at me and chuckles lightly.

"Olly, you need to breathe," he laughs, and Mom squeezes my hand across the table. I exhale and slap myself in my head. I'm so happy for her.

We all start eating, and Mom gives me an update on what had happened at the theater while I wasn't there – nothing huge though. Dad asks why, and Mom covers up for me by telling him that I have been ill. He sighs and starts talking about how it's the guaranteed season to fall ill. I chuckle. It's nice to have him back home.

CHAPTER THIRTY-FOUR

There are no longer any orange leaves on the trees, but a thin layer of white snow. My dark boots leave footprints on the little path. I glance around me.

"Olly, over here!" A voice shouts behind me. I turn around and notice her sitting on a bench a bit far away. Arden. She looks beautiful. I walk over to her.

"Hi, you look great... and healthy," I add, and she smiles with her eyes. I pull her into a hug.

"Thanks," she whispers into my shoulder and pulls away.

We both sit down on the bench. I look around the little park. There are other people here with their dogs and hot drinks. I lean back and focus on Arden. She's staring down at her gloves.

"Jaden and I kissed for the first time on this bench," she speaks quietly and gives me a weak smile. I stop breathing for a moment, and my heart starts beating a little faster. Shit. This is why she wanted to meet up. This is so uncomfortable, and I'm so guilty.

"I'm so sorry," I whisper back but can't get myself to look her in the eyes. He *finally* did it.

"We both know that it was the right thing to do," she says, "I have been prepared for this moment for so long, but somehow it still came as a shock for me." Tears begin to appear in her eyes, and she fiddles with her fingers on her lap. I look directly in front of me. She looks at me; I can feel it. I have to stay calm through this. I have a lump in my throat, but I hold back the tears. I don't have any right to cry.

"He's so in love with you. Do you know that?" she says, placing a hand on my shoulder. I turn my head, and our eyes meet. I nod slowly.

"How did you know about us?" I ask carefully. My voice is shaking. My palms start to sweat inside my black gloves.

"It wasn't hard... Just the way you two looked at each other, and the way you two always craved each other's company, made it obvious... but, mostly because I have never seen Jaden be more low than what he has been without you. He's always been acting like he's fine, but I'm not stupid. I've been close to him for a very long time. I can see it on his face when something is wrong," she says, drying her tears with her sweater sleeve that is sticking out from her winter jacket. I put my hand on top of hers, which is still resting on my shoulder.

"I don't know what to say, Arden," I whisper through my sobs.

"But, I do. Thank you." Her voice is low, and her eyes red. I move closer to her, and she pulls me into a hug. She's unbelievable.

"I really hope you two figure everything out and follow your hearts," she speaks, looking firmly into my eyes. I can't help but smile.

"I hope so too."

CHAPTER THIRTY-FIVE

The noise of people talking on the other side of the long red curtains makes me even more nervous. A little girl is all pale next to me, and her hands are shaking uncontrollably. She has the main role tonight. I take her hand, and she looks up at me. I give her a comforting smile, or as comforting it can be from another really nervous person. She smiles back.

The curtains are getting drawn to the sides, and I give her hand a quick squeeze before letting go and walking over to the piano standing at its usual spot. The crowd is applauding at the children standing in their positions. They're waiting for the people to get quiet so they can start the play. I look at the crowd; I see them all sitting in a long row... Jaden too. All of them are looking at the children, except Jaden; he's smiling at me. I quickly look away. Mom gives me a sign from backstage, and I start playing. My fingers shake before I hit the keys. He makes me nervous and calm at the same time.

The children are obviously nervous, but they do a great job. The crowd laughs at the jokes and applauds when they feel like it. I look around, not needing to read the notations because I have learned all the notes by heart. Jaden is still looking at me; I don't look away though. His eyes meet mine, and he smiles like a silly little child. I can't stop myself from doing the same, but I draw my focus back to the piano. I need to concentrate. It makes me so happy to see him smile.

Tonight, it is pure happiness I feel coming from him, and his lips, wow, they cannot stop smiling. I look up again and see Dad with his phone, taking pictures of me. Looking proud. I blush and keep my head down.

The children sing and dance for the last time before bowing to the crowd. They are all up and applauding. I stand up as well and walk over to the children. The little girl has tears in her eyes but smiles. I am happy she feels proud.

"Thanks for coming. We hope you enjoyed the show and would want to come again next year!" Mom concludes, and I catch Jaden's eye just before the curtains close in front of us.

We all hug, and the children leave to see their parents who are waiting for them outside.

"Are you coming? The others are waiting for us outside," Mom asks, and I follow her out of the building. Eleanor stops us and gives me a quick kiss on the cheek.

"You're so talented, Olly! I knew you could do it!" she exclaims, and Mom smiles at us. I thank her and blush heavily. She gives Mom a quick hug and compliments her work on the show before disappearing down the corridor. I look over at Mom, and she takes my hand.

"I'm so proud of you, honey," she whispers, and we stand here for a moment before leaving the building.

The others are sitting in the cars that are parked outside the door. Mom and I jump inside our car, where Sam and Dad are sitting. Charles starts driving, and Dad follows them down the road. We are all eating out together tonight. I'm really nervous about being around Jaden — the butterflies in my stomach go crazy. I haven't spoken to him for what feels like ages. Dad compliments my performance, and I thank him. I didn't expect everyone to be this supportive; I haven't done anything like this since I was very little.

Dad pulls up at *Brooks café* right behind Charles. Of course, we are eating *here*. I should've guessed that. We all jump out of our cars. The café is closed, so there are no actual guests tonight. Judy unlocks the door and holds it open for all of us. I enter last, and she gives me a soft smile before walking inside right behind me. A lot of tables have been put together to make one big table, and it is all decorated nicely.

Everyone finds a seat, and there are only two left. Of course. Two empty seats in front of Sia and Katy. The only ones who haven't taken a seat yet are me and Jaden, who is preparing the food in the kitchen. I sit down. Katy is playing with her fork and knife while Judy is telling us about the menu that Jaden has prepared. Charles and dad joke around, and everyone seems to be having a great time.

"Go in and talk to him," Sia suddenly demands in a firm voice, but her eyes look soft. I almost choke on the water. Katy giggles, and I look sternly at her for fun.

"My brother doesn't bite, I promise," the little girl whispers across the table, and I can't hold back a laugh. She's so innocent.

"You pinkie promise?" I ask, narrowing my eyes and holding out my little finger for her to take it, which she does. Sia giggles and smiles satisfied as I stand up and leave the table.

I walk behind the counter and stop to calm my nerves, before finally walking inside. Jaden is standing with his back turned to me and is checking the food in the oven. I lean against the wall next to the door and listen to his soft whistle – he looks so cute standing there in his element. I've missed him terribly. Maybe, I should leave before he sees me. I don't know what to talk to him about. His break-up with Arden? No. That's weird. The door opens behind me.

"Do you need help with anything?" It's Judy asking. Jaden turns around, and his eyes catch mine before hers. He smirks and waves her off.

"No thanks, Olly is being a great assistant," he chuckles, winking at me. I blush heavily, and Judy leaves the kitchen. He grabs a knife and cutting board from a cupboard and turns to look at me again. I can't think of anything to say, and my mind is numb.

"You can cut the salad," he offers, taking a step back from the counter to make space for me. I hesitate before walking past him. He puts some already washed salad on the cutting board. I keep my eyes down, trying to ignore his stare and calm my breathing. He turns around, and I can hear him stir the food in some pots standing on the stove.

"You were quite... amazing on stage," he suddenly speaks, and I turn around to look at him properly. My heart stops beating as he does the same. Our eyes meet. It is different now when he isn't as far from me.

"Thank you. Your opinion means a lot... to me," I almost whisper back. My cheeks are getting hot. So, I escape eye contact and turn around again. He doesn't, though.

"How do you want the salad to be cut? Thin or in chunks?" My voice comes out lower than expected, and I cough. Jaden places his hand gently on my spine. I gasp without much noise at his sudden touch. His breath hits the back of my neck, and my heart beats faster. I try to ignore it and start cutting the salad in random pieces. He chuckles behind me and leans against the counter next to me. I can finally breathe again as his hand is no longer resting on my back.

"I never actually volunteered for this," I laugh, biting my lower lip to suppress a smile. He gently pushes me to the side, and I leave him with the knife.

"No? Why did you come out here then? To talk?" he asks cockily. He cuts the salad with the knife in less than thirty seconds, and he puts it down on the cutting board.

"Your sisters forced me in here, actually," I explain, and he turns to look at me.

"Maybe... because I told her to send you" he says, and winks at me.

"Why?" I ask, not sure if I'm ready for the answer.

"Do you remember what I promised you after the fight with Adam?" he whispers, taking a step closer so that our noses are inches apart.

I obviously remember that night. "I said that when Arden gets healthy, I would break up with her," he says, making a checkmark in the air, "and then come out to my family," he continues and makes another checkmark. My eyes widen, and I can't find any words to say. I can't believe they know. "And finally be with you forever," he finishes, leaning closer, taking my lips between his. I smile against his lips, and he lifts me up before spinning me around. He puts me down on the ground again, and I pull him into a hug. We stand like this for a bit before Jaden slightly pulls his head away from my shoulder, and our eyes meet as they are only a nose length apart.

"Olly, do you want to be my boyfriend?" he asks, and I nod without hesitation. He brings our lips together, and I get pressed back against the counter behind me. I play with the fabric of his t-shirt, brushing it with my fingers. 'Happiness' cannot begin to explain the feeling that's running through me right now.

Charles suddenly shouts from outside to find out if the food is ready, and Jaden gives him a quick update before bringing his focus back on me. He gives me one last kiss and continues cooking.

I stand back as he prepares the food and puts it on plates. I get permission to help him with it. He tells me that he didn't get accepted for the professional soccer team and has dropped out of school, which comes as a huge surprise to me. I ask him what he's going to do instead then as we start carrying plates inside.

"I'm going to work here full-time until I can start on a cooking academy instead," he explains, looking around the café with glowing eyes. I guess this has always been his passion.

Throughout the meal, our thighs brush against each other under the table. I can feel the butterflies every time, mostly because Jaden glances at me with his pretty blue eyes and sends me a silly smile. I can't believe he's my boyfriend – he's mine.

"The food tastes amazing, Jaden. Maybe we should eat here more often," Mom says, and he thanks her. I would love eating here every night, knowing that his magic is sprinkled all over the food and that I'm only a couple of meters away from him, separated by a thin kitchen wall.

"I don't think I have ever seen you smile as much as you have today," Dad tells me, and I turn my attention from Jaden. His eyes move to Jaden and back at me. I blush, realizing how obvious I probably am.

"Yeah, it's been a nice day. Don't you think?" I ask, trying to move the attention away from myself.

"It's always a good day when the people I care about are happy," he answers, and Mom gives his shoulder a light touch. She gives him a peck on his lips quickly and then smiles at him. I glance around – everyone seems so much at ease.

Fingers suddenly traverse my thigh. He slides his hand in between my legs and lets the hand rest in the warmth. This isn't fair. He draws circles with a finger on my inner thigh. I run my tongue against the roof of my mouth.

"Are people ready for the dessert?" Jaden asks, getting up from his seat, his hand leaving the warmth of my thighs. Everyone nods and starts stacking the dirty plates.

"Is my assistant coming with me?" Jaden asks me, holding out his hands for me to grab. I blush but take it. Sam giggles, and Sia, who's sitting next to him, joins him. How can Jaden take everything so cool, and I'm here – turning into a strawberry.

I just step inside the kitchen, and our lips start touching. That's why he was hungry for dessert all of a sudden. I put my arms around his neck and start lightly pulling his short hair. He pulls me closer while taking a few steps backward until his back rests against the counter. He grins against my lips and pushes me against the counter next to us. He lifts me up and runs his hands up and down my thighs, the same way he did at Katy's birthday party in the bathroom. I leave kisses down his warm neck, and he moans softly against my curly hair. I feel his breath on me, and it makes an indescribable feeling rush through my body.

A cough interrupts us, and we both pull away quickly, turning to see who it is. Judy. She is standing with a stack of plates in her hands and has a huge grin on her face.

"So, are you official now?" she asks, moving her eyes from me to him. I look at Jaden, not sure if he's ready yet, but he just smiles back at me.

"We are," he answers, and Sia shows up behind her mom with a stack of plates too.

"Finally! I can't believe you two had to wait almost a whole year to realize that you're made for each other!" she exclaims, and everyone laughs around the table. The door is open, so they heard the whole conversation. We are both blushing and trying to hide our faces in each other's neck.

CHAPTER THIRTY-SIX

It's the 24th of December, and Christmas has suddenly turned into my favorite holiday, maybe because I'm around some of my favorite people right now. It smells amazing in the cottage. Jaden, the dads, and Judy are cooking the Christmas dinner for tonight, while Sia, Katy, Sam, Mom, and I have the honor of decorating the tree. I have Katy sitting around my waist so that she can reach a little higher on the tree. She's heavy, but it's alright. Sam is putting on the Christmas lights with a little help from Sia.

"Who wants to put the star on top?" Mom asks, waving it in the air. I shrug, look around, and meet Jaden's eyes.

"I think Olly should do it," he says, smirking at me. No one disagrees, so Mom hands it to me. It's made out of glass and embellished with silver glitter.

"I'm not tall enough," I explain, glancing at the top of the tree. Jaden chuckles and walks over to me.

"Then, jump up on my back," he offers, and I hesitate before counting down from three and leaving the floor. He does a little jump to readjust my sitting position. I gasp and take a firmer grasp of his dark gray sweatshirt. It's soft, and I feel like cuddling up to him. Then, I remember the job that I was given and the fact that everyone's watching us. Jaden takes a step closer, and I reach out.

My hand is slightly shaking; I know how much my mom loves the star. I put it in place with a little struggle, and everyone cheers. Now, it really feels like Christmas in here. I'm about to let go of him, but he holds on to my thighs and runs towards the stairs. I scream, fearing I'll fall down.

"We'll be back in a little bit!" Jaden shouts at the others and runs upstairs with me on his back. I tighten my grip around him until we get to our room, where he gently drops me on our bed.

"Shouldn't you help in the kitchen?" I ask, confused. He closes the door and lies down next to me on the bed. I turn to look at him; he turns too, and our faces are only inches apart.

"They will be fine. The food just has to simmer for a few hours, and then it's dinner time," he explains, removing a curl from my forehead before letting his hand gently run down my cheek. I grab it and plant light kisses all over it. He grins and moves a little closer. Our noses meet. I move my head slightly and we kiss, it was soft, almost innocent. Fireworks. Butterflies in winter? God I've become a hopeless romantic with this one. He places his hand on my hip and pulls me on top of him.

"Maybe we should jump in the shower then and put on our nice clothes?" I suggest, teasing him and pulling away to stand up. He sighs, throwing his head back on the bed. I walk into the bathroom and seconds later, hear his quick footsteps over the wooden floor.

"Babe? Can I at least join you?" he asks, showing up at the door opening. I can't hold back a laugh; he looks so desperate. I almost pity him.

"I never said you couldn't," I whisper back, and he quickly closes the door behind him with a wide smile on his pretty face. I'm so damn lucky.

I run downstairs. The table looks absolutely beautiful. I was meant to help my mom, but the shower took longer than expected.

"Olly, you look amazing!" Sia shouts from the fireplace, where she and her little sister are wrapping the last few drawings from Katy. I take a quick look at myself in the fridge; I don't look bad – a nice white shirt with thin blue stripes and black skinny jeans like always.

"It's Jaden's shirt. He thought I should try it," I explain and walk over to them. Katy quickly hides a present behind her, but I act like I didn't notice it.

"You look like a prince," Katy says, and I look back to find Jaden standing behind me. He *is* looking like a prince. His blond hair is styled; he's wearing an all-white shirt with a black suit that fits him perfectly. He comes closer and gives my lips a quick peck, not wanting to make a show for the others.

"Dinner is ready!" Mom shouts cheerfully from the kitchen, and we all find a seat. Jaden and I are, of course, sitting next to each other, so that we can hold hands underneath the table and just be close to each other. We all clink glasses.

A few hours later, Katy, Sam, Sia, Jaden, and I are all lying on the double bed in our room watching a Christmas movie, which is kind of boring because it had to be something Katy could enjoy. It's okay, because Sam is texting his crush Maya, and Sia is giving him girl advice. This is really funny. Jaden is stroking the skin underneath my t-shirt and listening to Katy's rambling about the movie. I don't think he minds though; he loves kids. It's so nice that we're all hanging out together like this.

CHAPTER THIRTY-SEVEN

Warm breath hits the back of my neck, followed by light kisses that leave shivers down my spine. I turn around and see Jaden lying behind me. It's dark.

"Merry Christmas," he whispers and plants a soft kiss on my lips. Sia is snoring peacefully on the other bed.

"Merry Christmas," I whisper back, cuddling closer to his warm chest; our legs tangled together. I can't believe it's Christmas morning; I feel like a little kid again. I haven't celebrated Christmas much living in the apartment, so it's magical being here in the cottage with the people I love. He runs his hand slowly up and down my side, and I keep my hand on his thigh, which is leaning against mine. His lips and nose touch my neck, and it tickles my skin. I feel so loved.

We are all downstairs, sitting on the couches by the fireplace. Charles finds the presents under the tree and hands out one present at a time. Katy is sitting between Sia's legs and is so excited; she's the cutest little thing. Sam and I are trying to unpack his new Nintendo with a scissor and knife. Jaden is massaging my back underneath my shirt. He's so sneaky; I don't think anyone notices him doing it all the time.

"Can Jaden and Olly get my present now?" Katy asks and jumps off the couch. She helps Charles find it under the tree, in between all the other presents. She has already given Sam and Sia theirs. Her small hands hold out the thin present in

front of us. Jaden grabs it and gives her a quick kiss on the cheek.

"You can have the honor of opening it," he says, passing it on to me. I carefully remove the wrapping paper and smile instantly when I see the colorful drawing. Jaden glances over my shoulder and lifts Katy up on his lap.

"This is beautiful," I tell her and bring her into a hug. She blushes slightly as Mom asks if they can see. I turn it around for everyone to see. It's a drawing of Jaden and me standing in front of a pink castle with crowns on our heads, surrounded by red hearts.

"Will you come and visit us in the castle then?" Jaden asks her, and she nods, her eyes lighting up. She jumps down from his lap and runs over to take her place between Sia's legs. Charles looks for the next present. I keep the drawing to the side and poke Jaden playfully on his arm.

"I can't wait for you to buy me a house like that one day," I joke, he laughs and rests his temple against mine.

"You're dreaming," he tells me against my lips.

"I think I am,"

ENDING

The wind tugs my sweater, and goosebumps form on my skin. Snow falls gently on the already white grass underneath my feet. There's ice on the lake; it's easy to breathe, and I feel at ease. I had to leave the others for a few minutes to fully understand what my life has become. I don't wake up feeling sick every morning, wishing for something better, because there isn't anything that can top this feeling – this feeling of freedom and profound love. Love – something that I thought wasn't an actual feeling; something pathetic that people would make up to make me feel shit about my life. But, it's real. It's scary, but it's real in the best way possible.

I can hear footstep behind me and light breathing. His arms wrap around my waist and pull me a little closer. He kisses my nape, and I close my eyes to just absorb the moment.

"Thank you," I hear myself whisper. He spins me around, and our eyes meet. He looks confused.

"Why?" he asks, locking his hands in mine.

"For fixing me," I answer, and he smiles.

"You fixed me," he says. He's in tears. My eyes begin to water too as I put my arms around his neck. We both lean in, and our lips meet. I feel like fireworks are going off around us. There are the violins, white doves, and all of that stupid pathetic jazz, which is actually so lovely. I can't believe this story will have a happy ending...

THANK YOU

Wuhu, finally laying the final touches on this novel. What a year! I'm so proud of the result and can't really understand the fact that it's available to purchase all over the globe.

Now, there are some people I need to thank:

Thanks to family, friends, and friends I call family. I'm very grateful for each one of you! You bring so much love and joy into my life.

A special thanks to four weirdoes: Sarah, Tobias, Mom and Dad. I will never find the right words to describe my love for you guys... You're always there to support and give constructive criticism when needed. You make my life amazing.

I have been lucky to have some teachers who made me a better writer and I need to get them some credit as well. So: Lise, Kirsten, Stine, Krista and Winnie thanks for the feedback and cheering words on my journey, it really means a lot to me.

Often the motivation to write just wasn't there after a long school day but I always knew where to look for the little push I needed. So thanks to my mentors from all over the world: Lilly Singh, Connor Franta, Troye Sivan, Olly Alexander, Kevin Hart, Gary Vaynerchuk, Alfie Deyes and Zoe Sugg. You're the proof that hard work pays off.

And the last person who I owe the biggest thanks to is myself.

This wasn't easy. It challenged your patience, work ethic, and self-confidence- but you made it. I can guarantee you that Caroline back in 4th grade dreaming of publishing a book one day is very proud of you! Keep dreaming, keep working hard.

www.ingramcontent.com/pod-product-compliance
Lightning Source LLC
Chambersburg PA
CBHW061522050726

47503CB00015B/2601